LAZY DAYS AT THE STABLES ON MUDDYPUDDLE LANE

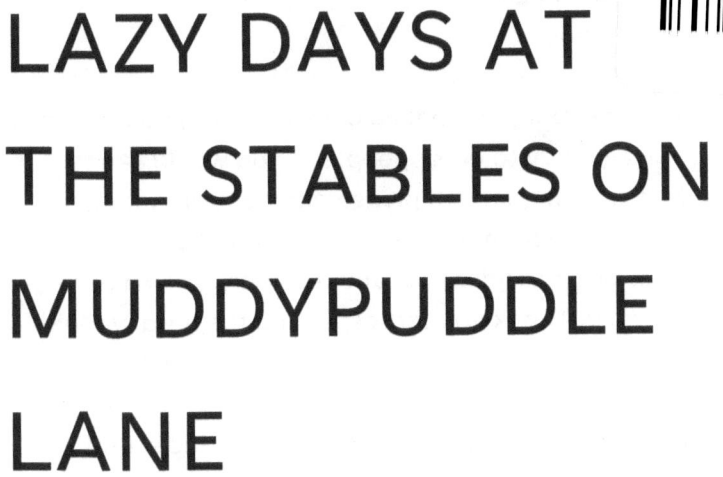
Heart-warming, uplifting romance

Etti Summers

CHAPTER ONE

Table booked at a suitably posh and expensive restaurant? **Tick.**

Taxi ordered? **Tick.**

Ring safely in pocket? **Tick**

Ashton shuffled nervously from foot to foot as he checked his appearance in the hall mirror. As usual, his hair was sticking up at the front and he smoothed it down. It immediately sprang back up. He was overdue a haircut, but he'd forgotten to go to the barber. He hadn't forgotten to buy a new shirt for the occasion, though. He'd debated whether he should wear a suit but decided against it – he didn't wear one if he could avoid it.

A car horn alerted him that his taxi had arrived. Checking yet again that the ring was in his pocket, he grabbed his keys and hurried out the door.

'The Wild Side in Picklewick please, but can we pick someone up on the way?' Ashton asked.

After giving the driver Lacey's address, he settled back in his seat and tried to relax. His leg jerked nervously, and he put a hand on his knee to hold it steady. The other began to jerk instead.

'Calm down,' he muttered under his breath, conscious of the taxi driver who kept catching his eye in the rear-view mirror.

'Special occasion, is it?' the chap asked.

You could say that, Ashton thought. 'Anniversary.'

'How many years have you been married?'

'We're not married.' **Not yet**. 'This is the anniversary of our first date.'

He had met Lacey outside a nightclub in Thornbury two years previously. She had broken one of her stiletto heels, and he had helped her limp home. She had been somewhat the worse for wear, so when she'd offered to take him out for a drink to say thanks, he hadn't been expecting to hear from her again especially since she didn't have his phone number. But she did have a fair idea of where he worked, because he had been wearing his Royal Mail uniform at the time. Her night out may have been drawing to a close, but his day had been about to start, as he had been on his way to begin his shift.

He had almost forgotten the incident, but was sharply reminded of it a few days later when he'd found her loitering outside the sorting office in the hope of catching him. She'd caught him alright – hook, line and sinker. They had been going steady ever since.

They didn't live together though, despite Ashton spending more time at her place than his own. At least, in the beginning he did, but that was until the early morning starts had begun to get to her. These days, he tended to return to his own little house when he had to be up at the crack of dawn, to allow Lacey to get a decent night's sleep. She wasn't a happy bunny when she was tired.

The taxi pulled up outside the terraced house she shared with a friend, and the driver beeped the horn. When there was no sign of her, Ashton got out and rang the bell.

Lacey opened the door after the second ring. 'Sorry, I couldn't find my shoe.' She hopped forward on one shoe-clad foot before catching hold of his arm and bending down to slip a strappy silver sandal onto her other foot.

They shared a smile as she locked up.

'You and shoes,' he said, shaking his head and opening the rear door of the taxi for her.

She got in, and he hurried around to the other side. 'Where are we going?' she asked.

'Somewhere nice.' Ashton caught the driver's eye again and gave a little shake of his head, warning him not to spoil the surprise by telling her.

The restaurant they were about to dine at was owned by celebrity chef Otto York, and Lacey had wanted to try it ever since it had opened. It had a sterling reputation, was always fully booked, and was eye-wateringly expensive.

It was also a fitting place to propose, Ashton thought, as he patted the ring in his pocket yet again before hastily dropping his hand to his side and hoping she didn't notice how nervous he was. He didn't want to spoil **that** surprise, either.

Ashton didn't do cheesy. He wasn't a hide-the-ring-in-the-bottom-of-a-champagne-flute kind of guy, and neither did he like the idea of putting it in the delicately flavoured wild bilberry cheesecake with the lavender biscuit base and rosehip compote drizzled prettily around the plate.

Instead, he waited for the coffee to arrive and topped up Lacey's glass with the sparkling rosé wine before he made his move.

'I've got something to ask you,' he began, his hand edging towards his trouser pocket.

Lacey had been relaxing into her seat, a contented expression on her face, but she seemed to stiffen and there was a guarded look in her eye.

It was now or never. Taking a deep breath, he eased the jewellery box out of his pocket and slid off his chair into a kneeling position. There was a sudden hush and Ashton was aware that every pair of eyes in the restaurant were trained on their table. With trembling fingers, he opened the box to reveal a sparkling square-cut diamond encased in gleaming platinum.

'I love you with all my heart, Lacey. Will you marry me?'

Everyone held their breath. And continued to hold it as the hush stretched into an awkward silence. Ashton watched as the wary expression in Lacey's eyes turned to one of embarrassment.

'Um... Can we, like, talk about this later?' she asked, glancing around and blanching.

Ashton felt the colour drain from his own face, only to return in a whoosh of dismay and mortification as realisation struck.

Lacey was turning him down!

Carla pushed through the crowded pub, craning her neck as she went. The place was hot and noisy, and her nose was assaulted by a hundred different perfumes, the smell of hops, and the lingering aroma of food from the buffet laid out at the rear of the room near the bar.

Carla loved it. She would love it even more if she could spot Yale.

He was the man who was currently making her heart sing and her insides perform somersaults. He was also her line manager, and the company they worked for didn't encourage fraternisation between management and staff, especially those staff whom a manager was responsible for.

Carla fully appreciated why, but it hadn't prevented her and Yale from 'fraternising' at every opportunity. She hoped to be able to get him on his own this evening so they could fraternise some more. It might be difficult though, because the reason she and many of her colleagues were at the pub was because one of their number (and a reasonably senior one at that, hence the good turnout) was retiring.

She and Yale hadn't made any arrangements to see each other after the party, but she was seriously considering inviting him back to hers later. The anticipation of making love to him for the very first time was making her quite giddy. It would take their relationship to the next level, and maybe they wouldn't have to sneak around as much. Or would the increased intimacy mean they'd have to sneak around even more? She bloody hoped not.

There he was!

Her heart lurched at the sight of him. Tall, classically handsome, even with the round spectacles (which Carla suspected he wore more out of vanity than necessity because it made him look intelligent), Yale was the sort of man most women – and many guys – looked at twice.

If (*when*) they took the next step and slept together, Carla wondered whether it might be an idea for her to transfer to a different department. But she loved what she did and loved the department she was in. Besides, any move would probably be a step backwards, as there wasn't an equivalent role to hers at the same level. Still, the insurance company they both worked for was large and new opportunities arose all the time, so it wouldn't hurt to keep an eye open. She had been a fraud investigation officer for a while, so she could even consider applying for a promotion.

Right now, promotion was the furthest thing from her mind. All she could think about was how sexy Yale looked when he laughed. He was currently chuckling at something one of the blokes in the credit department said, and she dearly wanted to go over and join in the banter, but she thought it best not to.

Yale continually impressed upon her the importance of not broadcasting their relationship, so she was careful not to give anyone cause to suspect that the two of them were anything other than colleagues. It made life difficult because she struggled not to let her feelings show when she was at work, but she could appreciate where he was coming from. He did her annual appraisal, checked her performance, and could even discipline her if necessary, so the last thing he needed was to be accused of favouritism. Which someone would no doubt do if they knew about them, despite Yale having never shown her any preferential treatment.

Carla bought a white wine spritzer and mingled for a bit, chatting with various people, yet she was always aware of Yale in her peripheral vision. Now and again he would casually pass by, close enough for her to smell his cologne, and one time his hand even brushed against hers.

A buzzing from her clutch bag made her reach for her phone, and she smiled when she saw who the message was from, smiling even wider after she'd read it. Yale had found an empty function room on the first floor and he wanted her to join him.

Carla's pulse fluttered as she anticipated a swift but passionate kiss out of the view of prying eyes. It looked like they would be able to grab a couple of minutes together after all.

After she meandered through the throng and stepped into a corridor leading to the loos, the noise level dropped significantly. Spying a staircase at the far end, she headed for it, glancing behind to make sure no one was watching. Gordon from sales was coming out of the men's toilet, but he didn't notice her, so she trotted up the stairs as fast as she could in her too-high heels.

When she reached the top and emerged into an expansive, empty room, Yale was waiting for her. Music, voices, and laughter floated up the stairs, but Carla felt disconnected from it.

His eyes glittered when he saw her and as he reached for her, she sank into him. His mouth found hers and he kissed her hungrily, his hands roving up and down her back, settling on the cheeks of her bum, pulling her close.

'Let's get out of here,' she murmured when they eventually came up for air.

'Can't.' His mouth found hers again.

They kissed for a few minutes more, then Carla broke away. 'Why not?'

'Got a wedding to go to tomorrow. Better not have a late night.'

Late night? Carla had been hoping he would stay **all** night, not merely for part of it.

Yale ran a hand through his hair, his fingers raking it into position, and Carla smoothed her dress, which had ridden up during their embrace.

He said, 'I need to go back to the party before I'm missed.'

'Another kiss?' she begged, hoping she would be able to change his mind about spending the night with her.

His grin was rueful. 'Can't get enough of me, eh?'

'Never,' she murmured seductively as she pushed him back against the wall and pinned him in place with her arms. She pressed herself against him and her eyes closed, as she anticipated another thrilling kiss.

'**Stop!** What the hell do you think you're doing?' he demanded at the same time Carla heard a woman cry, '**Yale?** What's going on?'

He shoved Carla away so violently that she staggered and almost fell. Regaining her balance, she turned her shocked face to the person behind her.

The woman was tall and slender, dressed to the nines, and had shiny, bouncy blonde hair. Even though her mouth was twisted in outrage and her eyes were narrowed into a furious glare, Carla could tell she was pretty.

Yale held out his hands in supplication. 'It's not what you think, Rachel. You've got to believe me.'

'Yale?' Carla was bewildered. Who was this woman? And who cared whether someone on the staff had caught them snogging? The company might take a dim view, but it was hardly a crime. Yale was seriously overreacting.

He turned to her, the sexy smile gone. In its place was disgust and contempt. 'Why can't you take no for an answer? How many times do I have to tell you I'm not interested?' He brushed past her, saying to the woman, 'I came up here to use the gents because someone had been sick in the ones downstairs.'

He jerked his chin, and Carla's confused gaze flickered to a sign at the far end of the room. It said **Toilets** and there was an arrow next to it.

'She must have clocked where I was going and followed me,' he continued, taking hold of the woman's arm and leading her towards the stairs. But before he descended them, he paused, turned to Carla and snarled, 'That's it, I'm done. No more Mr Nice Guy. I'm reporting you to HR for harassment.'

'What?' Carla's voice was faint. This couldn't be happening.

Yale shook his head sadly. 'There's no point in denying it and pretending nothing happened or that it was a misunderstanding. My fiancée witnessed your appalling behaviour.' He put his arm around the woman and ushered her down the steps. 'Come on, darling. I'm sorry you had to see that. What are you doing here, anyway? I thought you were in Walsall for the evening.' His voice faded as they reached the bottom, then disappeared altogether, lost in the laughter and chatter of the party.

Carla couldn't move. She was frozen to the spot, disbelief, horror, and heartbreak rendering her immobile. Then, as the realisation that Yale had a **fiancée** solidified in her brain, she slowly sank to the floor.

He had lied to her, had used her, and had toyed with her emotions. He was nothing but a cheating, slimy scumbag.

So why did her heart feel like it had been torn in two?

'You look awful,' Vicky announced as Carla slunk into the office on Monday.

Carla not only looked awful, she also felt it. After crying herself silly when Yale had left her alone in the empty room, she'd managed to stagger out of the pub, thankfully avoiding eye contact with anyone, and had made her way home to sob in the safety of her bedroom.

She had continued to weep on and off for most of the weekend, and by Sunday evening she had been a total mess, having not eaten or slept for forty-eight hours. Feeling nauseous but knowing she should eat, she had ordered a takeaway, managed to force about a third of it down, and had then collapsed exhausted into bed.

Getting up for work this morning had been hard, and despite her best efforts, she knew she looked hideous.

'You shouldn't be at work if you're not well, hun,' Vicky continued. She stroked her bump protectively.

'What I've got isn't catching.' Carla flung her bag and coat on her desk and dropped into her chair.

'Do you want to talk about it?'

'Yes, but not here.' She glanced around furtively. Yale's door was open, but he wasn't in his office.

She dreaded seeing him. This was going to be so awkward, and she felt the first fluttering of anger as she considered the position he had put her in. No wonder the bloody man didn't want their relationship to become general knowledge. He could hardly have broadcast it, considering he was already **in** a relationship. He had a fiancée, for pity's sake!

Her anger was accompanied by shame and bitterness. She wouldn't have gone near him with a barge pole if she'd had the slightest inkling he was taken, and she wondered whether anyone else knew he was engaged. Yale had only been working in the Birmingham office for a couple of months, having transferred from the Leeds branch, but that was no excuse for hiding a fiancée. There'd been no hint of it on the grapevine either, so she could only assume he had deliberately kept it quiet.

Vicky said, 'Shall we grab an early lunch? You can tell me all about it then.'

Carla guessed that Vicky would be shocked to learn that Yale was a two-timing arsehole. And she would be even more shocked when she knew it was Carla he was two-timing, as she hadn't told anyone, not even her best friend Dulcie, that she had been seeing him.

Deciding to get her head down and do some work (it would be an excuse not to look at Yale or acknowledge him when he appeared) Carla stowed her bag under her desk and started up her computer. She had got as far as logging into her emails when the phone rang.

It was an internal call and the news wasn't good. Mrs Bissett in HR wanted to see her. Now.

Carla bit her lip as she felt the remaining colour drain from her already wan cheeks. Had Yale carried through with his threat? She hadn't honestly thought he would. She'd assumed it had been bluff and bluster in the face of almost being caught in the arms of another woman.

Another woman… Carla never imagined that she would be the other woman. It made her feel ashamed and immoral.

Standing up abruptly, she sent her chair scooting backwards. 'I've been summoned to HR,' she announced when she caught Vicky's concerned glance. 'Shit and double shit.'

'I take it from your reaction, it isn't going to be good news?'

'No.' Carla scanned the office to make sure no one was listening. 'I've been seeing Yale,' she said.

Vicky's brow furrowed. 'Okay, it's frowned on but it's hardly a reason for HR to get involved.'

'There's more.' Hurriedly she explained what had happened at the party.

'What a rotter!' Vicky looked furious.

'Rotter?'

'I'm trying not to swear. I don't want the baby to hear.'

'No, of course not.' Carla straightened her shoulders. 'Wish me luck.'

'I bet it's about something else and not about that at all,' Vicky replied, trying to reassure her, but her tone lacked conviction.

Carla was expecting to see Yale in Mrs Bissett's office and was thankful when he wasn't. Still, she was nevertheless alarmed when the HR Manager informed her that an assistant would sit in on the meeting to make notes.

After being invited to sit down, Mrs Bissett explained the purpose of the meeting.

Carla struggled to take it in. The words 'allegation', 'misconduct' and 'investigation' lodged in her head, swirling around as she tried to make sense of them.

And when Mrs Bissett said, 'Possible disciplinary action,' Carla felt tears well up and threaten to spill over.

'I can't... It's not... It wasn't like that!' she blurted. 'If he's told you that I threw myself at him, he's lying. We've been seeing each other for the past month. As boyfriend and girlfriend.' As soon as she said it, she knew it wasn't true. How could he be **her** boyfriend when he was committed to another woman?

Hopelessly, not expecting to be believed, she continued, 'He's only saying that because his fiancée caught us together.' Oh, that sounded so bad when she said it out loud, even if it was the truth. Feeling the need to explain, she added, 'I didn't know he was engaged, honestly I didn't. He never told me, otherwise I wouldn't have...' She trailed off.

'May I stop you there, Carla. You'll have the opportunity to put your side of the story at a later date. This is just an informal chat to make you aware there has been a complaint and that you are under investigation. Furthermore, as you work in the same department as the complainant, I'm afraid we'll have to transfer you until matters are resolved one way or another.'

Close to tears, Carla tried to work out what she meant by 'one way or another.'

And when she heard that she was being transferred to sales, which she had little experience of and even less enthusiasm for, she was unable to contain her dismay. The tears she had been so valiantly trying to hold back, spilled over and trickled down her cheeks as she began to sob.

It wasn't fair! **She** wasn't the one in the wrong, yet she was being punished for it.

At the sight of her distress, Mrs Bissett showed a modicum of compassion and sent her home for the rest of the day. As far as Carla was concerned, it was the least they could do.

And the way she was feeling right now, they'd be lucky if she showed up tomorrow. Or ever again!

Carla stared at her phone's screen, seeing the concern on her mum's face.

'Have you spoken to anyone? Taken some advice?' her mum asked.

Carla nodded. It was mid-afternoon in Birmingham, seven in the morning in the Caribbean, which was where her mother currently was. She worked as a holiday rep for Silver Sands Getaways and, as the name suggested, she got away a lot. During the summer, Carla hardly ever saw her. She didn't see her all that often in the winter months, either.

The arrangement suited them both, especially since Carla still lived at home. At thirty years of age, she felt that she should have a place of her own, so this was the next best thing. Considering she didn't have a whopping great mortgage around her neck, it was probably better. The benefit for her mum was that the house was occupied whilst she was away.

Right this minute, Carla wished her mum was here, despite her not being able to do anything other than give her a cuddle and some moral support.

'I've spoken to my union rep,' Carla replied. She'd had a long conversation with a lovely man called Charlie, who had basically told her not to panic. But how could she not panic? She could lose her job over this, and the thought of going to work tomorrow, into a different department and doing something she was overqualified for, made her feel ill.

What was worse was that even if her colleagues didn't know what had gone on, rumours would be rife and she didn't think she could face the whispers behind her back and the speculative looks. If she had been allowed to remain at her own desk, she might have been able to ride it out. But not as things currently stood.

Her voice breaking, she said, 'I can't go back there.'

'Then don't.'

'But I **have** to. I can't resign. It would be seen as an admission of guilt.'

'I'm not suggesting you resign,' her mum said. 'I'm suggesting you take a leave of absence until this blows over.'

So that was precisely what she did.

CHAPTER TWO

It was surprising the amount of wildlife which could be found in urban areas, Ashton thought, as he left the house. To be fair though, Thornbury wasn't as urban as some towns he could mention, as it was surrounded by rolling hills and farmland, pretty villages and tiny hamlets.

It also benefitted from having a canal running through it, and that was where he was headed now, his camera around his neck. It was a substantial piece of kit, and he often attracted odd looks from strangers as they wondered why he was carrying such a large camera and what on earth he could be photographing.

This morning, he was hoping to spot a heron. They regularly fished in the canal on the outskirts of the town, especially in the early morning when it was quiet. Only the most resolute of joggers and the occasional dog walker were out and about at this time of day.

Sidling through a swing gate, he stepped onto the towpath and walked along it for a short distance until he found a suitable place to stop. The towpath was well-maintained, but the edges had been allowed to grow wild, and large trees and bushes lined the gravelled path. Wildflowers grew freely, and the hum of busy insects added to the birdsong and the quacking of squabbling ducks.

Slipping his rucksack off, Ashton carefully wriggled between two substantial bushes and took out a small folding stool, making sure it was steady on the uneven ground. He had also brought sandwiches and a flask of tea, but he didn't take those out just yet. He wanted to give the resident wildlife time to forget he was there first. Photographing wildlife took patience, and that was something Ashton had in spades. He could spend hours sitting on a riverbank, in a field, or on the side of a mountain without being bored.

Lacey hadn't understood. With the benefit of hindsight, he finally realised that she hadn't wanted to.

With peace settling around him as he blended into the undergrowth, Ashton's mind began to wander. He'd found himself doing that a lot over the past few weeks, which wasn't surprising considering his humiliation in the restaurant.

When Lacey had refused his offer of marriage, she'd said she wanted to talk about it later, but little discussion had been involved after he'd taken her home. She had clearly been embarrassed, and the surprise he had planned had come out of left field. As far as she was concerned, marriage had been the last thing on her mind. In fact, she was contemplating ending their relationship, and this made up her mind. Lacey may have been the love of Ashton's life, but he clearly wasn't the love of hers. And, he had discovered, she wanted more excitement than a mere postman could give her. Apparently, he wasn't ambitious enough, either.

Ashton hadn't been able to argue with that. He **wasn't** ambitious. He had no urge to climb the corporate ladder and no burning desire for greater responsibility because, along with the increase in salary, there would be an increase in stress. He liked his work-life balance just the way it was. Besides, he enjoyed what he did. He was out in the fresh air for a big part of his shift and getting plenty of exercise at the same time. He didn't want to be stuck behind a desk all day. He earned enough to pay his bills, with a bit left over for his hobby plus a meal out now and again and a couple of drinks down the pub.

Thinking of meals out made him cringe as he recalled the events of that night, and he vowed never to set foot in the place again. The staff had been lovely, but he had felt the weight of their pity as he'd paid the bill and left sharpish. And if it wasn't for the fact that Picklewick was on his round, he probably wouldn't have gone anywhere near the village again, either.

A flash of orange and turquoise caught his eye, and Ashton sucked in a breath. It was a kingfisher!

The bird plunged into the water, then flew onto an overhanging branch to eat its catch.

Ashton's camera whirred silently as it captured image after image. He zoomed in, the telephoto lens displaying the bird's gloriously iridescent plumage as it manoeuvred the fish into the right position to swallow it whole. Breakfast finished, it darted off peep-peep-peeping as it disappeared from sight.

Ashton let out a soft, delighted breath. What a treat! He couldn't wait to show Lacey the photos—

Reality threw a bucket of cold water over him as he remembered that he and Lacey were no longer together. And even if they were, she would have shown scant interest in his photography. The only photos she was interested in were those with her in them.

Crossly, he told himself to stop thinking about her. It didn't change anything and only served to make him feel even more sad.

These past few weeks had been awful, filled with misery and hurt, and today was no exception. He didn't think he could face going home just yet. He would stay here a while longer, because although they had spent more time at her place than at his, the house felt far too empty.

He could cope with the silence, but the loneliness in his heart was a different matter.

Dulcie was waiting by the door when Carla arrived at the farm, and as she held out her arms, Carla stepped into her embrace. 'Aw, you poor thing,' her friend said, hugging her tight, then called to her partner over her shoulder, 'Thanks for picking her up, Otto.'

'No probs. See you later,' Otto said, getting back in his car and driving out of the yard.

Carla hugged her back fiercely. 'I could have got the bus,' she protested. She had considered using her mum's car, but as she didn't drive often, she didn't feel up to a long journey on unfamiliar rural roads, especially when her head was 'in the shed' as her nan used to say.

'Nonsense! Otto had to go into Thornbury anyway, so it was no bother.'

'Are you sure you don't mind me staying with you for a while?'

'Of course not! You should have come sooner. I did ask you to.' Dulcie released her and slipped an arm through hers, leading her across the cobbled farmyard to the house.

A black cat ran up to them, almost tripping Carla as it wound around her legs.

'That's Magic,' Dulcie said. 'She seems to have adopted us. I think she's a stray.' She bumped the door open with her hip. 'Coffee? Or wine?'

Carla wasn't in the mood for alcohol. 'Coffee, please.' She plonked herself down on a kitchen chair. 'Thank you for having me. I don't think I could have faced another day on my own in that house.'

Dulcie gave her a stern look. 'I'm going to set a few ground rules, and the first one is that you have to stop thanking me. I'm your friend – that's what friends are for.'

Carla smiled sadly at her. 'Everyone descends on you when they've got a problem, don't they? Nikki, Maisie, your mum, and now me.' She barked out a laugh. 'At this rate there won't be anyone left in Birmingham. They'll all be here!'

'Do you blame them?' Dulcie pointed at the view through the window. 'Look at it! This place is gorgeous.'

'It is,' Carla agreed, accepting a mug of fragrant coffee. She had been travelling for ages, and this was very welcome.

Dulcie joined her at the table, cradling her own mug. 'I can't believe the investigation is dragging on for so long, even if that ratbag is out of the country. Surely they can carry on without him?'

'Apparently, he didn't give a statement, or whatever it was that HR wanted him to do before he went on annual leave. He's in Mexico currently.'

Dulcie gave her a shrewd look. 'Was this holiday already planned, or did he decide to flee the country because he didn't want to face the flak at work?'

'I'm not sure he had any flak to face,' Carla replied miserably. 'I'm the bad guy, remember? I'm the one who **'threw herself'** at him.' She did air quotes with her fingers. 'Vicky says everyone knows, despite it supposedly being confidential.'

'He's leaking it,' Dulcie said. 'He's going on the offensive and getting his version in first, so no one believes yours even though it's the truth.'

'I can't go back there. The thought of walking into the office makes me feel sick. Thank goodness HR agreed I could take leave until it's sorted out. Without pay, of course. But I don't care. I would happily live on fresh air if it meant I didn't have to go back there.'

'What will you do? Resign?'

Carla shook her head. 'I want to, but it'll make me look guilty.'

'Can they sack you?'

'Probably. Definitely, if they believe Yale. Which they will.'

Dulcie reached across the table and clasped her hand, saying gently, 'Don't you think it's better to resign, instead of being sacked? Especially if you've no intention of ever going back.'

Carla lowered her head. 'I don't know what to do,' she replied, her voice breaking.

'Whatever you decide, you can stay here for as long as you need.'

'You might regret saying that.' Carla's chin wobbled.

'Nah, the bright lights of Birmingham will lure you back eventually. How many times have you told me that Picklewick is a lovely place to visit, but you wouldn't want to live here?' She finished her coffee. 'Drink up and unpack your case, then I'll introduce you to the goats and show you how you can earn your keep.'

'Please don't tell me you want me to milk them,' Carla begged.

'Better! I'm going to do goat walks.'

'You're joking, right?'

'Not at all. You've heard of llama walks? Well, I'm going to be offering goat walks. Goats are nicer than llamas because they don't spit.'

'You want me to walk a **goat**?'

'Why not? They've got to start their lead training, and getting out in nature will do you good. You'll be the farm's official goat walker from now on.'

Carla almost wished she was back in Birmingham. Almost, but not quite.

Carla had seen goats before. The last time she'd visited the farm, Dulcie had been looking after the two goats belonging to the stables. Now though, Dulcie had eighteen goats of her own. **Eighteen!** She also had a flock of chickens, several cute bunnies, and a cat. How did she cope with all those animals, especially the goats?

Carla found out the following morning after Dulcie had shown her the changes she'd made since her last visit.

'I milk the adults every morning,' Dulcie said, rattling a bucket filled with something she called sheep nuts. It was ridiculously early, but Carla had been awake and heard Dulcie pottering around downstairs, so she'd got up. She was beginning to think she should have stayed in bed.

They were standing next to a gate leading to what Carla could only describe as a kids' play area – but for goats. As she watched the young goatlings jump and prance as they followed their mums, she wished she had half their energy. She felt like she had been steamrollered, picked up, then steamrollered for a second time.

Dulcie rattled the bucket again and opened the gate, careful to keep the treats out of the animals' reach. Tutting, she said, 'You know the rules, girls; you have to wait until you're in the milking parlour.'

Bemused, Carla watched as Dulcie shepherded the goats inside, before attaching the milking equipment to their udders. The goatlings didn't seem at all bothered as they trotted off to the barn for their own breakfast of fresh hay, bleating loudly with excitement.

Organised chaos was the best way to describe it, Carla thought. Dulcie was in her element, and Carla marvelled at how much her friend had changed since she'd won the farm. Once upon a time, Dulcie would have run away screaming if a goat so much as looked at her (in fact, Carla recalled Dulcie doing just that when a hand-reared sheep had demanded to be petted) yet look at her now. She was every inch a farmer.

She was so happy and so in love with what she was doing, that Carla felt a pang of envy. Dulcie was also madly in love with Otto, which gave Carla another pang. Once upon a time, she'd hoped that her relationship with Yale would lead to the kind of happiness Dulcie enjoyed.

Groaning inwardly, she told herself to stop thinking about him, but it was hard not to. If the investigation hadn't been hanging over her, she might have been able to put him out of her mind completely after the way he'd treated her She had initially thought she was heartbroken, but as the days had dragged into a week, and then a second, she'd realised that what she'd felt was infatuation, not love. As someone who dated a lot but rarely allowed a man to touch her heart, it had been a shock to discover how smitten she'd been. But she'd mistaken attraction, lust and the excitement of keeping their relationship quiet, for love.

Carla would never make the same mistake again.

Milking done, the two friends went indoors for a breakfast of scrambled eggs on toast, as the farm had an abundance of free-range eggs, courtesy of a small army of chickens. There was also a glut of juicy, ripe pears from the trees in the orchard, as well as punnets of glossy blackberries in the large fridge where the milk bottling took place. Dulcie had told her some of Otto's dishes in his restaurant featured the fruit. She explained that he obtained much of the produce he used in The Wild Side from the farm and its surroundings, including the spinach and other salad leaves growing in the veggie plot. As Dulcie had shown her around, Carla admired the couple's resourcefulness and ingenuity.

'How do you like the goats?' Dulcie asked, sprinkling salt on her eggs.

Carla swallowed a mouthful before she spoke. 'The little ones are cute.'

'It's their mums who will be walked.'

'Can't I walk the babies instead?'

'They'll play up if they're separated from their mothers. The adults are used to having halters on, so hopefully they shouldn't find going for a walk too stressful.'

'Couldn't you have had dogs instead? They **like** being walked.'

'I'm leaving the dogs to Maisie. Did I tell you she's opening a boarding kennel? Anyway, owning goats was your suggestion, remember?'

'I didn't think you'd do it. I was simply throwing ideas out there.'

'And that one stuck.' Dulcie grinned. 'Go on, why don't you take Cloud for a walk after breakfast? The fresh air will do you good.'

'With the whiff of goat in my nostrils? Hmph!'

'The view from the top is gorgeous.'

'You want me to walk all the way up the mountain?' Carla was incredulous.

'It's hardly a mountain. More like a hill.'

'I thought I was here for some rest and relaxation?'

Dulcie scoffed, 'The only time you relax is when you're sprawled on a sun lounger on a Mediterranean beach with a cocktail in your hand, and even then you're on high alert in case a fit guy walks past.'

Carla pressed her lips together. The thought of ogling any man right now turned her stomach. Sprawling on a sun lounger sounded good, though. Suddenly, she realised how utterly weary she was and how much the last couple of weeks had taken out of her.

She also realised she had come to the farm for a complete change of scenery, and hiking up the mountain while towing a goat was as complete a change as she could possibly get.

'Okay,' she agreed with a sigh. 'Saddle her up.'

'You can't ride her,' Dulcie warned, looking alarmed.

'I wasn't going to. It was just an expression.'

'I wouldn't put anything past you. You're always up for a laugh. My mum used to call you the wild one. I was the sensible one. Talking about being wild, how about we go out for dinner this evening? Otto suggested we go to the restaurant so he can cook you some proper food. He didn't think much of me shoving a supermarket pizza in the oven last night, although I thought it was a perfectly acceptable meal. We can come back here afterwards and crack open a bottle of wine. What do you say? I know it's not the party lifestyle you're used to, but it's the best I can do – unless you fancy a drink in The Black Horse. I've got to warn you though, it's bingo night.'

Carla wrinkled her nose.

'I didn't think bingo would float your boat,' Dulcie laughed. 'Wine and a natter back at the house, then.'

However, it wasn't the thought of bingo that Carla disliked. It was the thought of going out. She hadn't been out – as in a bar or a pub – since that night. Not only had Yale's deceit given her heart a knock, but her confidence had also taken a battering.

It didn't help that she'd had too much time to dwell on what she was doing with her life, and how it had gone so horribly wrong. One minute she had been having fun, enjoying her job, loving her social life, and with the prospect of being in a relationship with someone she really liked, and the next minute, everything had come crashing down around her.

The subsequent thinking and dwelling over the past two weeks had led to the realisation that all her friends were moving on with their lives, whereas hers hadn't changed in almost a decade. She was thirty and what did she have to show for it? She mightn't have a job soon, she didn't have a place of her own, and she didn't have anyone special in her life. Even Maisie, Dulcie's flighty younger sister, had settled down and was making a go of things.

Fed up with herself, Carla followed Dulcie as she went to fetch the goat. She'd read that llama walks were meant to lift the spirits and relieve stress and anxiety, so maybe walking a goat would be just as relaxing.

Somehow she doubted it.

I wonder whether goats are able to find their own way home, Carla mused as she gazed at the heather and bracken-covered hillside. The farm was down there somewhere, but she couldn't see it from here and she prayed she wasn't lost. Hence the hope that goats had similar homing instincts to pigeons.

She had stopped for a breather, one of many because this hill was steep, but Cloud didn't seem bothered that her nice comfy barn was out of sight. The animal was busy gorging itself on the surrounding foliage, as were her babies.

For the first ten minutes, Carla had been concerned that the goatlings would wander off (she really didn't fancy having to explain to Dulcie that she'd lost two of her precious goats), but she needn't have worried as they didn't stray too far from their mum. And while Cloud had tip-tapped obediently behind Carla as she had led her along the narrow dirt path, the babies gambolled and scampered amongst the heather.

They were incredibly cute and funny to watch. However, they soon realised from their mother's contented chewing that there was a smorgasbord of munchable leaves all around, and they quickly settled down to nibble at them.

As she watched them eat, she wondered how much further she needed to go. Would this do as Cloud's first proper walk? The goat had behaved herself, so did she need any more training?

Aside from the contented chewing noises, it was rather peaceful up here with just the wind and a bird call or two. The sun was warm and the springy heather looked quite inviting, so Carla decided to extend her breather into a proper rest and enjoy the solitude and the view.

It was a far cry from the noise of the open-plan office where she should have been this morning. The scenery was better, too.

Keeping a firm hold on the lead rope in case Cloud decided to make a break for it, Carla sank into the heather as her thoughts lingered on work, and she wondered what they were saying about her. She really should give Vicky a call to see how bad the gossip was and to reassure her friend that she was okay. She also wanted to find out whether Yale was back from leave yet.

Carla could feel her anger growing at the thought of that man going about his normal day while she was effectively in exile.

Did she miss work? Did she heck! Given a choice, she would rather be sitting on the side of a hill in the sun and watching goats eat grass, than be at work, but it was the principle of the thing. And also, the small problem of losing her job would mean no income.

Reflexively, she eased her phone out of the back pocket of her jeans and checked to see whether there was anything from HR. There wasn't, and she didn't know whether to feel disappointed or relieved. She desperately wanted to get this over with, but feared what would happen when it was.

Movement caught her eye and she stiffened. Was that a rabbit? Carla held her breath, keeping as still as possible. No, it wasn't a rabbit. It didn't have the ears for it. It looked like a cat, and was bounding and bouncing over the grassy tumps. Unusual markings, she thought, as it came closer – a brown back and white chest. Then suddenly it was gone.

She exhaled slowly.

Having lingered enough, she got to her feet. It was time to go back. She reckoned she'd been out here long enough.

Realising he was whistling, Ashton pressed his lips together to trap in the sound. Lacey had hated whistling. She used to say it 'did her head in,' and that it was tuneless, which he vehemently denied. He didn't for one minute believe his whistling was tuneless. In fact, as he was shoving letters and leaflets through the letterboxes on Hazel Road, he thought he had been giving a fairly decent rendition of **Sittin on the Dock of the Bay.**

Knocking on the door of number twelve and handing the young woman her parcel, it occurred to him that he no longer had any reason to suppress his whistling tendencies. He could whistle to his heart's content, and no one would stop him.

Pursing his lips, he gave an experimental toot.

'Someone's lively this morning,' the woman said.

She looked familiar, but so did most of Picklewick. Then it occurred to him where he'd seen her before. 'You're usually at the farm on Muddypuddle Lane, aren't you?'

'That's right. It belongs to my sister, Dulcie.'

Ashton slapped a palm to his forehead. 'Of course! Maisie, isn't it? I thought I knew you from somewhere. You look like her, too.'

'All us Fairfax kids look the same. Even my brother Jay, although he's more masculine.'

'I'm off up there in a bit,' he said, patting the Royal Mail bag which was slung across his body. Not that he had anything for Muddypuddle Lane in there, as those letters were currently in the back of his van.

'Do you want me to take them for you?' Maisie asked.

'Thanks for the offer, but I'd better not. It's against the rules.' He smiled. 'You could be anyone, and I've also got post for the stables and the cottage. Besides, I quite like driving up there – great views and I sometimes get to see some wildlife.'

'Yeah – Dulcie!' Maisie giggled. 'Don't tell her I said that.'

'I won't.' Ashton gave her a wave as he walked off.

It didn't take him long to finish his route in the village, and then it was time to hop back in the van and head off to Muddypuddle Lane. He had a couple of farms, isolated houses and businesses after that, before moving on to a small hamlet about two miles away. He didn't mind the deliveries being so far apart because he enjoyed the drive through the countryside, especially in the summer. Everything was bursting with life and was so lush and green. The sun was a welcome sight, and he wound down his window to let the breeze play over his face.

Slowing to turn into Muddypuddle Lane, he smiled as he saw the horses in the field. They were galloping, their necks arched and tails held high, and seeing them made his spirits soar. There was nothing quite as beautiful as a horse running free.

As he got out of his van at the stables, he breathed in the scent of horse. It wasn't an unpleasant smell, and when he saw an equine head poking over the top of a stable door, he paused for a moment to give its nose a stroke.

Letters delivered, it was the turn of the farm at the top of the lane next.

After handing Dulcie her post, Ashton was about to get back in his van when he saw a woman walk into the farmyard. She had a goat on a lead, closely followed by a pair of gambolling youngsters.

It wasn't the goats that gave him pause though, it was the woman. She was gorgeous – spiky dark hair, high cheekbones, big hazel eyes and a figure a man could lose himself in for days. Not only that, but he was certain he had seen her before.

'Made it back safe, I see,' Dulcie called to her. She turned to Ashton. 'This is my friend Carla. She's staying with me for a while.'

He took a second to find his voice. 'Hi.'

Carla smiled, instead of replying. It didn't quite reach her eyes.

'This is Ashton, my postie,' Dulcie said to Carla. 'You met him last time you were here, remember?'

Ah, that explained it. It was over a year ago, but he had a good memory for faces.

Carla looked at him, but there wasn't any recognition in her eyes. And why would there be? As Ashton recalled, the meeting had been a very brief one indeed.

He gave her a nod, and as he opened the van door he heard her say, 'I think I saw a stray cat. It definitely wasn't Magic.' She pointed up the hill. 'It was up there.'

Dulcie said, 'It's probably Walter's ginger tomcat. That creature is feral.'

Ashton got into the driver's seat and clipped in his seatbelt.

'It wasn't ginger,' Carla was saying. 'It was chocolate-coloured with white all down its front. It looked like it had lain in a pot of paint. It was really small though, but very bouncy.'

Ashton paused. It didn't sound like a cat. From Carla's description, it sounded remarkably like a stoat or a weasel. He'd only ever caught glimpses of a weasel, and he had never seen a stoat.

Vowing to return after his shift, he drove off down the lane. However, it wasn't the possibility of photographing one of the elusive creatures that caused the buzz of excitement in his chest – it was the possibility of seeing the woman with the troubled eyes.

CHAPTER THREE

'How was the goat walk?' Dulcie asked after the postie had driven off.

'It was good, actually.'

She smiled. 'I knew you'd like it. Can you do me a favour and take them to the field? I've got to get back to work.'

Carla felt awful. She'd descended on Dulcie without warning, so of course Dulcie had to work. As well as the farm, her friend had a 'day job' working for a large energy supplier, dealing with customer complaints, but there was an upside in that Dulcie was able to work from home. Carla didn't know how she managed to do both.

'What else can I do to help?' Carla asked.

'Aw, that's sweet of you, but Maisie will be here in a minute.' Dulcie shot her a meaningful look as she said, 'You won't believe how much she does around the farm. She finally seems to have found something she enjoys. I'm going to miss her when the kennels are up and running.'

'When will that be?'

'Early next year, Adam estimates. Bless him, he's doing most of the work himself, as well as running his business. It's a good thing he's so brilliant at stuff like that. He can turn his hand to anything.'

'What does Maisie do on the farm?' Carla was still wondering how she could help.

'Milking, bottling, soap making, egg collecting, rabbit feeding – anything and everything.'

'Surely there's something I can help with? I can't just sit around doing nothing.'

Dulcie reached out to stroke her arm. 'You don't have to, honestly. You've had a tough time of it lately. Just relax and put your feet up.'

As Carla watched her walk back to the house, tears pricked her eyes. Dulcie was the best friend ever, and Carla wished she still lived in Birmingham. It wasn't the same without her. When Dulcie won the farm, Carla had been convinced Dulcie would soon realise life in the sticks wasn't for her. But to her surprise, Dulcie had taken to it like a duck to water (after an initial blip or two) and was now incredibly happy. She was also madly in love, and Carla couldn't help wishing that she could find a love like that. She had begun to think she might have found it with Yale, but look what a rat he had turned out to be.

Carla returned Cloud and her babies to the field to join the other goats, and watched them for a while, enjoying their antics as the little ones played together. Then she dawdled back to the house.

When she got there, she discovered Maisie had arrived and was about to start making soap.

Maisie greeted her with a hug. 'Long time, no see,' she said.

'It's been a while,' Carla agreed. 'I hear you'll be running a kennel soon.'

'Yeah, who'd have thought it!'

'Not me.' Carla grinned at her. 'Look at you, adulting at last.'

Abruptly, she sobered as she realised that Maisie's lifestyle was now far more adult than her own. Maisie was the one with a house, a business plan, and a partner. Whereas Carla was still living with her mum, her boyfriend had turned out not to be hers at all, and she wasn't sure whether she still had a job.

Maisie gave her a sympathetic look. 'Dulcie told me about your stinker of a boyfriend.'

'But he wasn't **my** boyfriend, was he? He was someone's **fiancée.**'

'Stop beating yourself up. You weren't to know.'

'Is that what I'm doing?'

'Uh-huh.'

'But he could cost me my job.'

'So? Get another.'

'That's easy for you to say,' Carla retorted.

'Because I've had loads of them?' she laughed. 'Doesn't that prove my point?'

'But I like my job.'

Maisie shrugged. 'In that case, you'll have to fight for it.'

Easier said than done, Carla thought. How could she fight when she didn't have a leg to stand on? Yale had made sure of that.

'Why the goggles?' Carla eyed the pair in her hand with mistrust. They weren't exactly fetching.

'Lye is basically sodium hydroxide,' Maisie explained. 'It's horrid stuff. You don't want to get it on your skin, and definitely not in your eyes.' She gave her a pair of black, heavy-duty rubber gloves. 'You'll need to put those on as well.'

'Why use it at all, if it's so horrid?'

'When it's mixed with fats and oils the chemical reaction leaves no residue, so it's perfectly safe. In fact, you can't make soap without it. Well, you **can**, but it's not classed as natural soap.'

Carla frowned. 'Do you mean that the soap I washed my face with this morning contains lye?'

'It does. Plus goat's milk, coconut oil, olive oil and fragrance.'

'You know an awful lot about it.'

'I've been making soap for a couple of months now, but there's still a lot to learn.'

Carla examined the equipment and ingredients laid out on the workbench. She and Maisie were in one of the sheds next to the milking parlour. After being informed that it used to house sheep, Carla was convinced there was still a whiff of the woolly animals in the air. Her eyes roved around the room, noting the fridge and freezer, the racks of shelves with colourful bars of soap on them, and the table with an old bookcase behind which held the finished products, packaged and neatly labelled.

'Where do you sell it?' Carla asked.

'Online, although we do have the occasional customer who buys it direct from us when they pop up to the farm for their milk and cheese.'

'You and Dulcie have a proper production line going on.' Carla was filled with awe.

'We have. In fact, Dulcie's hoping that by the autumn, she'll be able to give up the day job and concentrate on this. She's just started making candles too, as another string to her bow.'

Maisie was interrupted by the sound of a vehicle pulling into the yard, and she went to take a look. When she returned ten minutes later, she said, 'That's another satisfied customer. Dulcie gets people popping in all the time to buy milk and cheese, and when I mentioned we had a glut of pears, she bought a bag of those as well. There's a lot of surplus produce, so it's good she can make few pounds from it.'

'I don't know how she manages to fit it all in. How does she cope with people just turning up out of the blue if she's working?'

'Luckily, she's got me most of the time, but when the kennel is up and running I won't be around much, so I've no idea how she'll manage.' Maisie put her goggles on and slipped her hands into the rubber gloves, indicating that Carla should do the same. 'You won't believe how inconsiderate some people are, though. Last week, she had someone knocking on the door at eleven o'clock at night, wanting to buy milk for their bedtime cocoa.'

'Why doesn't she have a proper shop?'

'Not enough hours in the day, can't afford the rent – to name two reasons. Anyway, when she does give up her job, she'll want to be on the farm, not in the village, and renting a shop would eat into her profits.'

Carla waited a moment before she donned her goggles. 'I wasn't thinking about a shop in the village. I was thinking about her having a shop **here**. I noticed she keeps the milk and cheese in the bottling shed, the soaps in here, and the fruit in the barn. If she had everything in one place, with a proper counter, display units, and set opening times, it would be much easier for her. If customers are already dropping in ad hock, it makes sense to have them arrive when it's convenient for Dulcie, and there's also the likelihood of add-on sales if all the items are together.'

Maisie was staring at her, her eyes huge beneath the goggles. She shook her head slowly. 'Carla Mason, you're a genius! Why didn't we think of that?'

When they eventually began making soap, Carla was smiling. She mightn't be able to sort out her own pathetic life, but at least she could be useful to someone else.

Ashton drove into the yard and tucked his car to one side, out of the way of any farm vehicles which might be trundling back and forth. Then he got out, slung his camera around his neck, feeling the familiar weight of it, and patted his pockets to make sure he had the lenses he might need. He'd attached the telephoto lens before he'd left the house, but he mightn't keep it on the whole time he was out. It depended on what caught his eye and how he was going to photograph it.

Locking his car out of habit, he headed across to the house to speak to Dulcie. But it wasn't Dulcie who answered his rat-a-tat knock, it was her friend, Carla.

On seeing her, Ashton's pulse quickened. She really was gorgeous, and although he wasn't ready to start dating again (it would be quite a while before he put himself out there), at least it proved he might be one day.

'More post?' she asked, then she clocked the camera and her eyebrows rose.

'Hi, is Dulcie in? I need to have a quick word.'

'Yeah. Hang on a minute.'

She turned away, presenting him with her profile, and he tried not to stare at the curve of her cheek or the way her long lashes curled almost to her brow.

She yelled, 'Dulcie, your postman wants a word!'

Ashton heard Dulcie shout that she would be there in a second, which left him and Carla gazing awkwardly at each other.

'You've got a big camera,' she said, then to his amusement she blushed furiously. 'That's not a euphemism, by the way.'

He held back a smile. 'I didn't think it was.' He stroked the long lens absently, then realised what he was doing and snatched his hand away. Oh flip, now he was blushing.

Carla smirked. 'What's your speciality? Or shouldn't I ask?'

'What? **No!** I don't—! He sighed. 'Wildlife.'

'You're here because of the cat, so am I right in thinking it wasn't a cat at all?' She studied him, and he felt the weight of her stare on his face.

'Probably not. From your description, I'd say it was a stoat or a weasel.'

She shook her head. 'I doubt it. It was tiny.'

'You'd be surprised how small they are. Squirrel sized.'

Her eyes widened. 'Really?'

Dulcie appeared in the doorway. 'Hi, Ashton. Is anything wrong?'

'Not at all. I wondered whether I could park my car in your yard? I'm off for a walk, you see, and—'

'He thinks the cat I saw this morning might be a stoat or a weasel. He wants to photograph it.' Carla sounded excited.

Dulcie's gaze dropped to his chest and the camera sitting there. 'You're a photographer?'

'In my spare time.'

'Any good?' she asked.

'Not bad. Hardly professional level, though.'

'If you manage to take a couple of snaps of it, will you show me?' Carla asked.

Snaps? He tried not to take offence. 'I will,' he promised. 'But the likelihood of seeing it is small.'

'**I** saw it.'

'Right place, right time,' he replied mildly.

Dulcie suddenly asked, 'Is photography just a hobby, or do you take on paid work?'

'Not as such. I have sold a couple of photos, though.' He tried to gauge why she wanted to know.

'I wonder whether you could take some shots of the farm for our website? I'll happily pay the going rate.'

'I'd be delighted to, but there's really no need to pay me.'

Dulcie scowled at him. 'That's no way to run a business.'

'I'm not running a business. I do this for fun.' He gently tapped the camera.

'I'll pay you in kind, then,' she said, shooting Carla a look when Carla giggled.

Ashton refused to meet Carla's eye. 'There's no need,' he reiterated.

'There absolutely is!' Dulcie was insistent. 'How about some fresh produce? We've got pears, eggs, milk and cheese, and I could add a couple of punnets of blackberries. Oh, and how about soap? Perhaps your girlfriend would like to take a look at our website and choose some.

We do candles, too. Better still, how about a nice romantic meal for two in The Wild Side?'

She was gazing at him hopefully, and Ashton tried not to flinch. He had no intention of stepping through The Wild Side's door ever again. Not after the last time.

'I, um, don't have a girlfriend.' He glanced at Carla as he said it, then hastily looked away.

Dulcie said, 'Sorry, I thought you did. My mistake.'

'We split up.'

'That's a shame. Would your mum like something instead?'

'The fresh produce is fine,' he replied, not wanting any but guessing that Dulcie wasn't going to take no for an answer.

'Great! I'll leave a note with my number on under your windscreen wiper, and we can chat about it tomorrow or the day after, if that's okay?'

'That's fine.'

'We could do it now, but we're going out in half an hour and I need to get ready. We're having dinner at The Wild Side.' Her eyes widened. 'You're welcome to join us.'

He caught Carla's surprised expression out of the corner of his eye. Even if he did consider accepting Dulcie's offer, he got the impression that Carla wouldn't appreciate him being there.

'I'm not really dressed for it but thank you anyway.' He glanced over his shoulder at the hillside behind the house. 'Thanks for letting me park my car here, I appreciate it.'

Dulcie said, 'It's no bother. Next time, don't ask. If I see your car in the yard, I'll assume you're off photographing something. And don't forget to give me a call.'

'I won't,' he promised. He was flattered she'd asked. Although, considering she hadn't seen any of his work, she might wish she hadn't. However, as he walked briskly up the path, he realised he was very much looking forward to showing Carla what he was capable of. No, not **Carla**, he amended – **Dulcie**.

Ignoring his mental slip of the tongue, he pushed on up the hill – he had a small, elusive mammal to capture on film.

Carla twiddled the stem of her wine glass, growing a little exasperated.

'You thought Ashton was hot when you visited last time,' Dulcie pressed. It was the second time she'd mentioned it.

'I don't think so now, okay?'

'Why not? He looks the same as he did before. He hasn't changed in the slightest.' Dulcie waved her glass in the air and wine sloshed out. Otto looked bemused.

'Maybe not, but I have.'

The three of them were enjoying an early dinner in The Wild Side, Dulcie enjoying it more than Carla and Otto combined, judging by the amount of wine she'd consumed.

Slurring her words, Dulcie said, 'You know what they say – the best way to get over one man is to get underneath another.'

'No thanks.'

'But he's cute!' Dulcie took a slug of her wine, and Otto gently took the glass out of her hand. 'Oi! What are you doing? That's mine.'

'You're tipsy,' he said.

'I know. Isn't it wonderful?'

'You won't think it's wonderful tomorrow morning when you're dealing with shouty, sweary customers.'

Carla said, 'She always was a lightweight.'

Dulcie looked affronted. 'I'm not!' She turned to Otto. 'Tell her I'm not.'

'She is,' he agreed, laughing.

Dulcie scowled and poked her tongue out. 'I'm not speaking to you. Go and do something cheffy and leave us girls to talk about girly stuff.'

Otto stood up, grinning. 'I'll send someone over with a couple of coffees.'

Dulcie tracked his progress to the bar. 'He's lovely,' she sighed.

Envy nibbled at Carla once more. She was delighted to see Dulcie so happy and in love, and would give anything to have that for herself.

'Do you think he's cute?' Dulcie asked.

'What? Otto? Er... I haven't really thought about it.'

'Not Otto, you dipstick – Ashton.'

'Oh, we're back to that, are we? Can we please stop talking about your postman?'

'Okay, but I think he fancies you.'

Carla rolled her eyes. 'I don't care if he does. Have you forgotten the reason I'm here?'

Suddenly Dulcie didn't seem quite so tipsy. 'No, I haven't. But I don't believe Yale was the love of your life, and I certainly don't believe you're heartbroken.'

Her comment made Carla pause. 'You're right, he wasn't and I'm not. He could have been, though.'

Dulcie snorted. 'Yeah, if he'd had a personality change. Anyone who behaved the way he did, is a creep.'

Carla had to agree. Admittedly she had been upset at how he'd deceived her, but she was over that now. She was still upset, but not about him – she was far too worried about losing her job. Yale could go to hell, as far as she was concerned. But that didn't mean she wanted another man in her life. It would be a very long time before she would get back on the dating horse again. She had too much going on to even consider it.

You win some, you lose some, Ashton thought as he made his way back down the hillside to his car. Two hours of sitting motionless in the bracken hadn't revealed even a glimpse of a stoat. However, he'd shot some lovely images of skylarks, a vole, the fattest bumblebee in the world, rabbits playing, and a slinking fox in search of his supper. So it hadn't been all bad.

Dusk was now falling and it would be dark soon, so it was time to make a move. He was absolutely starving, and thinking of food reminded him of Dulcie's offer to dine at The Wild Side this evening. Although his emotions were telling him he had been wise not to take her up on it, his stomach was yelling at him that he should have done. Despite never wanting to set foot in the place again, from what he could remember, the food had been delicious. No wonder, considering Otto York was a

Michelin-star chef. Maybe one day he would be able to face going back.

As he neared the farmhouse, Ashton's thoughts turned to the photos Dulcie had asked him to take, and he began to scan his surroundings for suitable subjects.

The sun had almost dipped below the hills on the opposite side of the valley, and the sky was bathed in pink, peach and gold. Directly below him was the field of sunflowers. He had passed the nodding yellow blooms on the way up the hillside, but he'd been focusing on the possibility of spotting the stoat or weasel and hadn't paid them much attention.

He noticed them now, though. With the setting sun highlighting them, the flowers positively shone. Before he knew it, he had lifted the camera.

Hopefully, he would get a few good photos for Dulcie.

Then he spotted something and froze.

A stoat was weaving through the long stems, its sinuous body the most gorgeous shades of chocolate: milk chocolate on its head and back, white chocolate on its throat, chest and belly, and the unmistakable dark (almost black) chocolate tip to its tail, which indicated it was a stoat and not a weasel. He was close enough to see that all four paws were also white, and the animal looked as though it was wearing tiny socks.

Praying it wouldn't spot him, Ashton zoomed in. He must have taken fifty photos before it disappeared, and he let out a slow satisfied breath.

This is what he lived for; this was what gave him joy and made him complete – not a job, or money, or things. **This.** Lacey had never understood.

As Ashton returned to his car, his soul filled with the wonders of nature, he made himself a promise that the next woman he gave his heart to, would love this as much as he did.

CHAPTER FOUR

Carla's heart was in her mouth as she eyed the contacts list on her mobile. Would Vicky be at her desk by now? And even if she was, did Carla want to speak to her? What if Vicky told her something she didn't like?

Aw, heck, Vicky was her friend; she absolutely should call her, even if the news from work wasn't the best. Anyway, Carla had hiked halfway up the mountain to get a signal because the mobile reception was so bad at the farm. She'd multi-tasked though, having brought one of the goats with her. She figured she might as well make herself useful, and keeping out of Dulcie's way this morning was also a good idea. Carla was glad she hadn't drunk as much as her friend; the poor girl looked rather green around the gills!

'Can you talk?' was Carla's opening line when Vicky answered the phone.

'Carla?' she whispered. 'Hang on, I'll go to the medical room. There's never anyone in there, and if someone does come in I'll hold my bump and groan a bit.'

Carla heard her friend's muffled voice as she greeted her co-workers, then she heard the lift ping, and knew that Vicky was in the corridor. The sound of a door opening and being firmly closed, was followed by heels clacking over a tiled floor.

'Okay, I can talk now,' she said. 'How are you? What's going on? Have you heard anything from HR?'

'I'm fine. I'm still at Dulcie's.' Carla had messaged Vicky before she'd left

Birmingham to tell her that she was staying at the farm for a few days.

'I thought you might be. But how are you really?'

'Okay, I guess. Angry, mostly. I feel so stupid.'

'Don't. It's not your fault. It's Yale's.'

'Is he back from his holiday?'

'Not yet. There's a rumour going around that he needed to take additional time off to recover from the trauma.'

'Trauma? What bloody trauma? I'm the one who is traumatised. The—' Carla bit back the rude word she had been about to call him.

Vicky said, 'Don't worry, no one believes it. He's not lying on a psychiatrist's couch, he's lying on a sun lounger on a Mexican beach. With his fiancée, obviously.'

'Obviously.' Carla's reply was pure sarcasm. 'I actually feel sorry for her. She doesn't know what she's letting herself in for.' She hesitated, then asked in a small voice, 'What's everyone saying about me?'

'Nothing bad. Everyone knows you wouldn't throw yourself at a man, especially not one who's already taken.'

Carla was momentarily buoyed up by the news, but it didn't last. 'I don't suppose it matters what they think, it's what HR believes.' It took an effort to rally, but she managed it, saying, 'How about you and Bump? Are you okay?'

'We're doing well.' Carla could hear the smile in Vicky's voice. 'I can't wait to go on maternity leave. Eight working days, then I'm out of here, and one of those is a training day so that doesn't count.'

'Are you still adamant that you're not coming back after you've had the baby?'

'Definitely not! At least, not for long. I'll be damned if I'm going to pay back any maternity pay. I'll have to check out the rules and regulations, so I might have to work for a few weeks. But that's it. After that, I'm done.'

'I don't blame you.' Carla could imagine how hard it would be to leave her baby and go back to work.

Vicky said, 'I'd better get back to my desk before someone comes looking for me. Keep in touch, yeah?'

'I will,' Carla promised, and as she said goodbye she wondered whether Vicky would have already begun her maternity leave when she came back to Birmingham for the hearing. She wished HR would get a move on, as the suspense was killing her. The sooner she knew that she had definitely been sacked, the sooner she could move on.

What she was going to move on to, was anyone's guess.

When Carla returned from her walk, Dulcie was sitting at the kitchen table with her head in her hands. Dulcie's mum, Beth, was also there.

Beth got up to give her a hug. 'Men!' she cried. 'There're all bath plugs.'

Carla smiled. 'Bath plugs?'

'You know what I mean. I have to be careful what I say these days, what with our Sammy, and little Amory at the stables. Little pitchers have big ears.' Beth stood back. 'Let me look at you.' The woman's gaze swept her from head to foot, and Carla tried not to cringe under her scrutiny. 'You're too skinny,' she announced. 'And you look worn out.'

'Thanks.' Carla didn't think she looked that bad; a little tired maybe, but that was the stress.

Beth turned to Dulcie. 'She does, doesn't she?'

Dulcie lifted her head. Her eyes were dull, and her normally healthily tanned skin was more of a grey colour. She groaned and dropped her head again.

Beth said, 'Serves her right. She forgets that she's getting older. At eighteen, you can bounce back from a hangover in a matter of hours. At thirty, it takes a day. When you get to my age, it can take a week and there's no bouncing involved. How's your mum keeping?'

Carla blinked at the abrupt change of topic. 'She's good, thanks. In Saint Lucia at the moment.'

'Tell her I said hello.'

'I will.' Carla and her mum messaged each other several times a week. It was often easier than phoning, as there was nearly always a time difference between them.

Beth bustled around making cups of tea and laying out a plate of biscuits, as they caught up on their news. Gradually Dulcie perked up, but there was still some way to go before she was back to her usual self. And when her phone rang, she winced.

Carla smirked, feeling rather virtuous, and left her to it. She'd spotted Maisie through the kitchen window, and went outside to see if she needed a hand. She'd enjoyed the soap making yesterday. It was very different from what she usually did, and had helped take her mind off her problems.

By the time Beth called them in for lunch, Carla had made several blocks of soap on her own (under supervision) and was feeling rather pleased with herself. She was also ravenous, not used to being on her feet as much.

Over a goat's cheese salad with new potatoes that had been slathered with lightly salted butter, the three Fairfax women discussed business while Carla listened.

She was fascinated to see how well Beth and her daughters got on, because the girls had been a bit of a handful when they were younger, and Beth had often been at the end of her tether.

Carla supposed it was only to be expected, considering she'd been a single parent with four kids to raise. The eldest, Nikki, lived in the village with her partner and son, Sammy. Jay, the next eldest and only boy, now lived in New Zealand, whilst Maisie had also relocated to Picklewick earlier in the year, Beth following shortly after.

Dulcie said, 'Carla's come up with a brilliant idea. She suggested we open a farm shop.'

'In Picklewick?' Beth asked.

'Here, on the farm. I can't afford to rent a shop in the village and I haven't got the time to man it, either. Not even when I give up the day job.' She glanced at the clock. 'Which reminds me, I start my shift in twenty minutes and Ashton is supposed to be calling in to take some photos of the farm for the website. Mum, do you think you can show him around?'

'Can't, sorry. Walter has an appointment at the hospital, and then we've got a macrame class at the community centre.'

'Maisie, how about you?'

'Adam has a delivery of bricks coming, and I said I'd be there to receive it. If you ask Ashton to come later today or tomorrow—'

'I can show him around,' Carla interjected. 'Tell me what you want him to photograph, and I'll point him in the right direction.' How hard could it be? The farm wasn't that big, and it wasn't as though Dulcie had hundreds of animals or tonnes of produce.

Dulcie pulled a face. 'Sorry about what I said last night. I know you're not ready to jump on the horse again.'

Maisie said, 'I didn't know you could ride?'

'I can't,' Carla replied. 'It was metaphorical.' She held up a hand, anticipating Maisie's next question. 'Don't ask.'

'If you're sure you don't mind,' Dulcie said doubtfully. 'You're supposed to be here for some R and R, not as unpaid labour.'

'I'm sure. Unless there's something else you need me to do?'

'It's all in hand, I think.' Dulcie checked with Maisie, who nodded.

Beth stood up and began collecting the empty bowls. 'I'll just stick these in the dishwasher, then I'll be off.'

Maisie got to her feet. 'I'd better be off, too. You know what delivery drivers are like. They estimate to be there between two and four, but I'd hate for it to be early and miss it.

Dulcie went to prepare for her shift dealing with unhappy customers, leaving Carla wondering what to do with herself until Ashton arrived. It was lovely out – warm and sunny, autumn not yet having made an appearance – so she decided to take a book into the orchard. She had quite enjoyed sitting in the heather yesterday, and hoped the peace and solitude would do her good.

After all, as Dulcie had pointed out, being at the farm was supposed to give her some respite from recent events. If that meant lazing around in the sunshine for an hour or two, that's what she would do.

Carla was fully engrossed in the uplifting romance she was reading (courtesy of the bookshelf in Dulcie's living room) when the sound of a vehicle coming up Muddypuddle Lane jolted her out of the story.

Checking the time, she realised it was probably Ashton, and she hurried to intercept him before he interrupted Dulcie by knocking on the farmhouse door.

He didn't see her at first, and she took a second to study him as he emerged from his car. Dulcie was right – Carla **had** referred to him as hot during her last visit and she could see why. Taller than her five-foot-seven by several inches, he was lean but had muscles in all the right places. His short sandy hair curled a little, and he was clean-shaven, with the loveliest blue eyes. She remembered thinking that he reminded her of a young Robert Redford.

'Hi.' His voice broke into her thoughts, and she realised he had caught her staring. 'Dulcie is expecting me,' he added.

'Er, yeah, she asked me to do the honours.'

'Okay, cool.' He reached into his car and carefully lifted out his camera and a small satchel-type bag which he slung over his shoulder.

'Did you see the stoat?' she asked, and was taken aback by the smile that lit up his face. He had **dimples!**

'I did. Want to see? It's better if we go into the barn,' he said and Carla raised her eyebrows, only relaxing when he explained, 'It's too bright out here to see the screen clearly.'

She followed him into the relative gloom of the barn's interior and waited until he was ready. She assumed he would hand her his camera, but he passed his mobile phone to her instead. 'My camera sends them straight to my phone. Do you think Dulcie might like to see them?' He glanced at the farmhouse, his expression hopeful.

'I'm sure she would, but she's working right now. Which is why you've got me.' Carla pulled a face in self-deprecation.

'No worries,' he said.

But Carla wasn't listening. She was too busy scrolling through the images on his phone. Damn, he was good! He'd captured the essence of the creature she'd seen perfectly. She couldn't believe how clear the picture was. It was like looking at a photo taken by a professional.

She studied each one intently, noticing the animal's whiskers, the play of light and shadow over its fur, and the bright beady eyes. Then she scrolled some more, and when the sunflower meadow came into view, she sucked in a sharp breath.

'Are they okay?' Ashton asked, and she looked up from the screen to see his worried face.

'They're brilliant!' she cried. 'Absolutely flippin' brilliant.' She angled the screen. 'This one is perfect for Dulcie's website. She's going to love it!'

'I hope so.' He looked relieved. 'Where shall we start?'

'In here?' she suggested. The barn was home to several adorable bunnies. 'Or maybe we could take them outside? Dulcie has a pen that can be moved around.'

'Perfect.'

There was a momentary awkward hesitation on both their parts, and it was only when he made no move to catch any of the rabbits that Carla realised he was expecting her to catch one.

Oh, crumbs.

The pen was in the orchard, just by the gate, and Carla was thankful that it wasn't far because the rabbit was squirming and wriggling. She popped it into the pen, glad to be relieved of the little creature.

'Do you think we can move the pen?' Ashton asked.

'Why?' She wasn't being awkward; she genuinely wanted to know.

'Because I'd like to get a shot of the rabbit without the pen in the picture. Maybe we could put it over there?' He pointed to an apple tree with lavender growing near the base of the trunk.

Carla could immediately see how the new location would work. The rabbit she had picked was the cutest: lop-eared with black and white fur that would stand out well against the lavender flowers, and the green foliage would hide the metalwork.

She picked the bunny up and held it whilst Ashton moved the pen.

'Make sure it's secure,' she advised, remembering Dulcie telling her that rabbits were excellent escape artists, which was one of the reasons they weren't left on their own outside for long as the naughty little creatures often tried to dig their way out.

The new location seemed to please the rabbit. It immediately settled down to nibble on a dandelion and Ashton wasted no time taking several shots. He was soon done and ready to move on to the next subject.

'Goats,' Carla announced. 'Let me pop this little fella back first.' She caught the rabbit, cradling it in her arms as she planted a little kiss on its fluffy head, then quickly returned it to the barn.

When she came back, she found Ashton busily photographing fruit. The trees in the orchard were laden with ripe pears and plums, although the apples weren't ready for picking just yet. On the other hand, the blackberries were definitely ripe. The shiny black fruit glistened in the sun, and Carla's mouth watered as she thought of blackcurrant crumble with lashings of golden custard.

They reached the goats' field and she was quiet for a while, letting Ashton concentrate, but the silence felt strained (although he didn't seem to notice) and eventually she felt compelled to fill it.

'Have you always been a postman?' she asked.

'Not really. I was a child once.'

'Ha ha, very funny.'

He grinned at her, revealing those dimples. 'Yes, I've worked for the post office since I left school.'

'Do you like it?'

'I do.'

'Why?'

'Dunno, really.' His attention was firmly on the camera, but she noticed his knuckles whitening as he tightened his grip and wondered why her question had caused such a reaction.

Carla persevered. 'Is it because you're outside a lot?'

'Partly.'

'Do the early starts give you more time to do this?'

He paused, holding the camera away from his face. 'I still do a forty-hour week.'

'But not nine to five?'

'No.' He lifted it back to his face. 'How about you? What do you do?'

'I work for an insurance company.'

'Doing what, exactly?'

'I'm a fraud investigation officer.'

'Do you like it?'

'Yes, it's interesting.'

'Are you from Birmingham?'

'I am.'

'Do you like it there?'

'Not as much as I used to. Do you like living in Picklewick?'

'I don't live in Picklewick. I live in Thornbury. It's a town about nine miles away.'

'I know it.'

'Yes, I do like it there. As towns go, it's not too big and it's got everything I need.'

'Like what? Pubs, restaurants, shops?' she guessed.

'A canal and good links to the countryside.'

'Do you live on a boat?'

He chuckled. 'No, I live in a regular house, but the canal is a brilliant place for wildlife.'

'Why photography?'

He put the camera down to his side. 'Why so many questions?'

Carla shrugged. 'Just making conversation.'

'I love photography because I can't paint and I want to capture some of the magic. Most people see a sunset, but few see a kingfisher or an otter in the flesh.'

'You're incredibly good. You've got a real talent.'

'Meh, anyone can take a decent photo.'

'I can't.'

'I bet you can.'

'Seriously, I can't. I've got a pretty good camera on my phone, but the photos usually come out blurry, or I've not noticed a lamp post coming out of someone's head.'

'You can teach yourself how to compose photos.' He pointed to one of the goatlings who was on top of the climbing frame.

'See that little one? If you took a photo of it now, it should be good because most of the animal is visible, and there's grass and sky for the background.' He slipped his hand out of the camera's strap and offered it to her. 'Give it a go.'

'**Me?**' Carla was incredulous. 'What if I drop it?'

'You won't.' He sounded certain, so she took the camera, holding it tightly. Then she relaxed her grip, fearful she'd break something with the strength of it. There were so many dials, buttons, and numbers, and she had no idea what they were for. Was she supposed to do something with them, or could she just point and shoot?

'Go on,' Ashton urged.

'Just like that? I don't have to twiddle or turn anything?'

His smile was indulgent. 'You can, if you want, but let's take one step at a time, eh?' He leant in, and she caught a whiff of his aftershave. He smelt lovely. 'Just look through there, and press this button,' he said.

'That's it?'

'Pretty much.'

Carla glanced around. What should she take a photo of? The goat on the climbing frame had jumped down and she bit her lip uncertainly. One of the animals was lying in the sun, its jaws working from side to side as it chewed. Hesitantly, she brought the camera up to her face and closed one eye to peer through the viewfinder. She gasped as she zoomed in on the goat's nose.

'I can see the colour of its eyes,' she whispered. Taking the camera away from her face, she stared at the creature, marvelling at the detail the telephoto lens revealed. 'It's like magic.'

Ashton chuckled, and Carla realised how daft she sounded. 'I mean, I know what zoom lenses can do – I'm not stupid – it's just... I've never looked through one before. It's nothing like the zoom on my phone.'

'No, it isn't.'

She put the viewfinder to her eye again, closing the other. The goat wore a dreamy blissful expression on its face, one that she envied. She pressed the shutter button.

'Can I see?' He moved closer to her, his chest against her arm. 'You can see the photo you've just taken by looking at the LCD screen.' He pressed a button, and the image appeared. Carla had captured the goat's expression perfectly.

'Not bad,' he said. 'Not bad at all. See, I told you that you could do it.'

'Can I have another go?' she asked.

'Absolutely. What else does Dulcie want me to photograph?'

Dulcie had only given Carla the briefest of briefs, so Carla wasn't entirely sure. She paused, imagining what might capture her interest if she were a customer, and what might persuade her to visit the farm. Natural, organic, and nature were the buzzwords that came to mind.

'Chickens,' she said. 'And eggs. People might like to see where their eggs come from.' She was thinking about the farm shop. 'And then the bottles of milk, the cheese, and the soaps.'

Ashton said, 'What if I take a few, then you can have a go? And as I take each image, I'll explain what I'm doing and why. But I must warn you, not every photo is a great photo. Everyone takes duds, me included, so don't expect it to be perfect every time. And before I shut up, I'll just say one more thing – it takes practice to take a really great shot. Lots and lots of practice.'

Ashton's passion for photography was clear, and it was catching. Carla could certainly appreciate what he saw in it, especially when it came to photographing animals.

She wished she'd thought to whip her phone out yesterday and take one of the stoat, but the creature would probably have disappeared by the time she'd got it out of her pocket. Anyway, her photo wouldn't have been half as good as Ashton's.

She could practice taking photos whilst she was here, she mused, as she led him towards the chicken coop in the hope of finding one of the free-range birds lingering nearby. It would give her something to do when she wasn't helping out on the farm. And it might be nice to dawdle through the fields looking for things to photograph.

She must admit that she'd felt better after sitting in the orchard with her book, so maybe Dulcie was right, and she needed time to recuperate. Finding out that your boyfriend already had a fiancée, being dumped, and that you might be about to lose your job, was enough to fray anyone's nerves.

CHAPTER FIVE

Ashton turned his pillow over, seeking the cooler side, and sighed in frustration. It was strange that when he had been with Lacey, he'd often felt exhausted by nine o'clock if he'd been at work that day. Yet since they'd split up, he spent half the night tossing and turning. If only he could have been this awake, Lacey mightn't have—

It was pointless thinking that way. She'd known he was a postman when they'd started dating, and had been aware his job involved early starts, so she could hardly have expected him to be the life and soul of the party when he had to get up at the crack of dawn.

Ashton checked the time. Twenty-past ten, and he was still wide awake.

Was there any point in lying there getting crosser and crosser because he couldn't fall asleep? Or should he get up and do something useful?

He decided to get up.

Pushing the bed covers aside, he swung his feet to the floor and padded downstairs in his boxers. He may as well look through the photos he'd taken today, and if they were any good, he'd email them to Dulcie.

He had also asked Carla for her email address so he could forward her the images she'd taken. He'd only had the briefest of scans through them when he'd arrived home because he had been more focused on food, so he'd left checking the images for another day. But as he couldn't sleep, he may as well look through them now.

Ashton sat at his makeshift desk (aka the table in the living room) and lifted the lid on the laptop. As he waited for it to start up, he decided to make a coffee.

Quietly, he slipped into the kitchen and filled the kettle, wincing at the sound, before remembering that he could make as much noise as he liked. He had become so accustomed to creeping around so as not to disturb Lacey, that it was now second nature.

He snorted softly – they say opposites attract, but perhaps night owls and early birds were a bit **too** opposite. Then there was her inability to appreciate how important photography was to him, and his bewilderment at her insatiable desire to watch soaps and her fascination with reality programmes. Yeah, total opposites.

After making the coffee, he grabbed a packet of oaty biscuits and returned to the living room, eager to see the photos, and clicked through them slowly, dunking a biscuit as he did so.

When he came to the photo Carla had taken of the goat, he paused. It wasn't bad at all he thought, then carried on looking at the rest.

He became so engrossed in what he was doing, that it wasn't until he'd neared the end of the photos did he realise there had been a couple of occasions where he hadn't been able to tell whether it was he or Carla who had taken an image, and it made him smile. She had been so adamant that she couldn't take a good photo, and he was delighted to be able to prove her wrong.

Ignoring the time (it was getting to the point where it was hardly worth going to bed), Ashton emailed the photos to Carla and Dulcie, adding **'I told you so'** and a smiley face emoji to Carla's. He hoped she would be pleased with her efforts and that seeing them would give her the confidence to take better photos.

Ashton stretched out his back and rolled his shoulders. He'd better get some sleep. But as he was finally drifting off, it wasn't Lacey who was in his thoughts, as she had been every other night since the split – it was Carla and the sweet look on her face as she'd cuddled the rabbit.

To her surprise, Carla found she was enjoying her regular goat walks before breakfast, and after just a few days she wasn't nearly as breathless walking up the hill. She was starting to fit into the slower pace of life at the farm and felt better for it.

When she entered the kitchen, Dulcie was whisking up eggs in a bowl. 'Good, you're back. I'm making scrambled eggs for breakfast. Would you like some?'

'Yes, please.' She was hungry. 'Can I do anything?'

'You could pop a couple of slices of bread in the toaster.'

'On it.'

Soon afterwards, she was sitting opposite Dulcie and tucking into her breakfast. Swallowing a mouthful, she asked, 'Is there anything you want me to do today?'

'Why don't you take a day off?'

'**You** don't.'

'It's my business, my farm. You're here to relax.'

Relaxing sounded good, but Carla knew she would feel guilty. She couldn't just sit around while Dulcie and her sister worked so hard.

'Actually, there **is** something you could do,' Dulcie said after a second. 'You could pop into the village and do some market research for me.'

Intrigued, Carla asked, 'Such as?'

'Have a mooch around the shops and see how they display things. I want to get some ideas.'

Carla felt a surge of excitement. 'Does that mean you're going ahead with the farm shop?'

'Otto and I talked it over, and we both think it's a great idea. It can't hurt to have a dedicated space to display the goods properly, and having set opening times will be a godsend. Eventually, I hope to have an online ordering system, so people can pay and collect.'

'Wow! You really are expanding, aren't you?'

'That's the plan. The farm is almost at the point where it pays for itself, and I'm hoping this will give it the extra push.'

Carla was pleased for her. She remembered how out of her depth Dulcie had felt when she'd first won the farm, and how she had considered selling up and moving back to Birmingham. It was wonderful seeing her so enthusiastic.

A trip into the village would be a welcome change, and she was looking forward to mooching around the shops. She also liked the idea of doing market research, especially as she had a vested interest in the venture, since the farm shop had been her suggestion.

'Can I get you anything while I'm out?' she asked after nipping upstairs to change and checking she had her car keys, purse and phone. As well as looking around the shops she might treat herself to a coffee and a cake.

Dulcie was staring at her computer and smiling. 'Ashton has sent the photos through. They're amazing. Take a look.' She scooted aside so Carla could see the screen.

'Oh, wow. They **are** good.'

Dulcie was grinning. 'In his email, he said that you'd taken a couple of them, and they were just as good as his.'

'He said that?'

Her friend's nod was emphatic. 'He did. And I must admit, I can't tell which ones are yours.'

A glow of pride warmed Carla's insides, and she grinned back. He'd asked for her email address, and she wondered whether he'd sent her anything, so she took her phone out of her bag.

He had! And when she read the 'I told you so' comment, she laughed out loud and showed it to Dulcie.

'To think he's done all this for nothing,' Dulcie said. 'He's definitely one of the good guys. I feel I should thank him in some way, but I don't know how. A dozen eggs and a bag of pears isn't enough. And he didn't seem keen on a meal in The Wild Side.'

Carla thought hard. 'Apart from photography, is there anything else he's into? I'm thinking maybe tickets for a concert or a football match?'

'I've no idea. I don't know anything about him, really. Just his name, what he does for a living, and that he lives in Thornbury. And he's single.'

'Oh no you don't, lady.' Carla gave Dulcie a warning look. 'I'm not going there.'

'Yale didn't break your heart,' Dulcie reminded her.

'No, but he's put me off men for a while.'

'I'm not suggesting you marry Ashton,' Dulcie replied. 'I'm just wondering where my love-them-and-leave-them friend has gone.'

'I'll let you know when I find her,' Carla retorted. The situation with Yale had caused an internal shift, and she had become more wary and less flighty than she'd been, but surely that wasn't a bad thing?

Dulcie's attention returned to the computer screen. 'Maybe I could get Ashton a voucher. I believe there's a photography shop in Thornbury which might do vouchers or gift cards.'

Carla said, 'Why don't I pop into Thornbury instead of Picklewick? If the shop sells them, I can pick one up.'

'That would be great. Thank you.'

It was the least Carla could do, considering Dulcie and Otto's generosity in letting her stay with them. Not that she'd seen a great deal of Otto because he was at the restaurant most of the time. However, Dulcie had assured her the situation would change as soon as he'd trained up a head chef and hopefully he could take a back seat, and he and Dulcie could spend more time together, especially if she gave up the day job.

Right now, Carla was wishing she could give up **her** day job, but unfortunately she had no other strings to her bow. Her bow had one solitary string on it, and she had a feeling it was about to snap.

After another quick scan of her emails to make sure she hadn't missed anything from HR or the union rep, Carla slipped her phone back into her bag, resolving not to think about work until she had to. She much preferred to think about her trip to Thornbury.

InFocus was a serious camera shop with serious equipment in the window, and Carla drew in a sharp breath at the equally serious prices. Good gracious, cameras weren't cheap, were they? If she had realised how expensive they were, she probably would have been too scared to touch Ashton's.

Her eyes roamed over the shelves as she tried to find the one Ashton owned, but they all looked much of a muchness and she was soon confused. And as for the lenses... Blimey, there were so many, and all of them had indecipherable strings of letters and numbers in their descriptions.

A shelf of second-hand equipment caught her attention. The items on it were considerably cheaper. This is the way forward, she thought, then pulled herself up. Anyone would think she was contemplating buying one. How daft would that be, considering she mightn't have a job soon and needed to hoard her pennies.

Realising that work had intruded into her thoughts once more, she walked up to the counter and the middle-aged man standing behind it. He had what appeared to be a camera in front of him, but she wasn't certain because it was in bits.

As he looked up, she said, 'Do you sell vouchers or gift cards?'

'I most certainly do.' He gestured to a small stand next to the till. Each little card had the most exquisite image on it.

She selected one, not caring that it was more than the amount Dulcie had suggested. Carla would cover the additional cost herself. She might need to keep a careful watch on her bank balance, but the boost to her confidence that Ashton had given her by his act of kindness yesterday was worth the expense. Dulcie was right, he **was** one of the good ones. At any other time, she might have been tempted to get to know him better, but not right now. She had too much going on to think about becoming involved with anyone, however brief the involvement might be.

After she'd made her purchase, Carla didn't immediately leave the shop. She wandered around it instead, peering into the locked glass cabinets, trying to recall the make of Ashton's camera.

Nikon, that was it, she remembered, and moved towards the cabinet with a Nikon sign above it.

'Are you looking for something in particular?' the man behind the counter asked.

'I was just curious. I was with a guy yesterday who had one of these. I've no idea which one, though. How do you choose?'

He came out from behind the counter. 'It depends on what you're looking for, how much you want to pay, and what you want to use it for. When people start out, it's normally the price point that has the greatest influence, but not always. What do you currently use?'

'My phone.' Her tone was sheepish.

'But you'd like to get into photography on a more serious level?' he guessed.

'Um, I don't know.' Emboldened by his kind eyes, she scrabbled around in her bag for her phone and clicked on the email Ashton had sent her. 'I took these yesterday,' she said, showing him the screen.

'With your phone?' He sounded incredulous.

'No, on Ashton's camera – he was the guy I was with.'

'Ashton? That wouldn't be Ashton Clarke, would it?'

'Yes. Do you know him?'

The man laughed. 'He's probably my best customer. He's here more than I am, which says a lot considering I own the place.' He pointed to the second shelf down from the top. 'That's his latest camera. It's a mirrorless one.' The man was gazing at her as though she was supposed to know what that meant, so she nodded sagely despite having no clue. 'It's his pride and joy,' he added.

She clocked the price on the ticket and her eyes almost popped out of her head. Bloody hell! If she'd known what it cost, she **definitely** wouldn't have touched it.

Had he trusted her that much? Or was money no object and he could afford to replace it if she'd had butterfingers?

The shop's owner provided the answer. 'Ever since that model came out, he's been eyeing it up. You wouldn't believe how pleased he was when he was finally able to buy it. He was like a kid on Christmas Day.'

Carla would like to hear more, but someone entered the shop and from the way the owner greeted them they seemed to be regulars, so she thanked him and left. It was time to complete the second half of her task in Thornbury, and a phone was a better option for this than a camera.

Trying to be circumspect and not make it obvious that she was taking photos, Carla wandered from shop to shop, paying particular attention to a greengrocer, a delicatessen, and a shop that sold bath bombs, lip balms and other fragranced items along the same lines as the things Carla made with her goat's milk. She lingered for a while in each, trying to make it look like she was talking on her phone, and when she thought she'd taken enough, she retreated to the nearest cafe for a well-earned coffee and a sandwich.

It was getting on for lunchtime, and Thornbury was busy. The cafe was no exception, so she was glad when she managed to bag an empty table by the window. She would enjoy people-watching whilst she ate.

She had just finished her prawn sandwich and was debating whether to have a second cup of coffee, when a Royal Mail van pulled into the kerb alongside a post box on the opposite side of the road. Seeing it reminded her sharply of Ashton, so it was a shock when the man himself got out.

Without thinking, Carla leapt to her feet, grabbed her bag and shot outside. Darting between the traffic, she hurried across the road.

Ashton had emptied the post box and was about to return to his van when she said, 'Hi,' somewhat breathlessly.

'Hello.' He smiled at her, dimples out (or should she say 'in'), and she beamed back. 'Retail therapy?'

'I'm running a couple of errands for Dulcie. Thanks for the photos. I can't believe how well they turned out. It must be the camera.'

'Not necessarily, although having good equipment does help. But some people can have all the gear and still have no idea.'

Carla shook her head. 'In my case, it was definitely the camera. I can't take a decent photo on my phone for toffee.' She hoped the ones she had taken today for Dulcie were okay. She should really have a quick flick through them to make sure before she went back to the farm.

She said, 'Dulcie was delighted with the ones you took.'

'I'm glad.'

There was an awkward pause. Carla didn't know what else to say, and she guessed he was probably keen to get back to work. She nodded at the envelopes he was holding. 'Got long left?'

'An hour. A couple more stops, then it's back to the depot. Are you off home now?'

Home, as in the farm on Muddypuddle Lane. Carla briefly wondered what it would be like to actually **live** there, and the thought was rather appealing. Recalling how she'd felt on her first visit when she'd reckoned it was nice for a short getaway, but she wouldn't want to live anywhere so rural, she was quite surprised. Maybe one day, when she had a husband and children, she would seriously consider living the good life in a village like Picklewick, growing vegetables and taking the kids on long walks in the countryside.

Dream on, she snorted to herself. The chances of her finding the love of her life anytime soon were minimal. But something had to give, because her party lifestyle was starting to lose its appeal, even more so since her friends were settling down with mortgages, partners, and babies.

She snapped back into focus as she realised Ashton was waiting for a reply. 'Not yet,' she said. 'I'm going to buy myself a camera.' She hadn't realised that's what she was going to say, until she'd said it.

'You are?' He looked delighted. 'Which one?'

Carla shrugged. 'I've no idea. I'll have to rely on the owner's advice and hope he doesn't fleece me.'

'Were you thinking of buying it from InFocus?'

'I was.'

'Barney won't fleece you. He'll give you good advice.' Ashton hesitated. 'Would you like me to come with you?'

'Yes, please, that would be great. If you can spare the time.'

'I've always got time for anything to do with photography. Do you mind waiting an hour until I finish work, or do you want to go another day?'

'Let's do it today,' she replied, ignoring the inner voice telling her that she was being ridiculously impulsive and she shouldn't be spending money on a luxury item like a camera when she mightn't have a job next week. Because, for the first time since that fateful night when Yale had shown her his true colours, Carla's heart didn't feel quite as heavy, nor her future seem quite so bleak.

Ashton couldn't wait to finish work. He always felt a surge of anticipation when he was about to pay InFocus a visit, but today he was practically hopping from foot to foot with excitement. The knowledge that he had introduced someone to the delights of photography, gave him such a boost.

Not wanting to pop into the shop in his uniform, Ashton ran home. Thankfully, he didn't live far from the depot, so he was home, showered, changed and back in town in less than half an hour. He had arranged to meet Carla at Rossi's Cafe near the town hall, and as he approached he worried that she might have gotten fed up with waiting and left.

His relief when he saw that she hadn't was greater than it should have been, considering he hardly knew her and they were only going shopping.

She hadn't spotted him yet — her eyes were on her phone — and he studied her through the cafe's window as he walked up to the door. She was smiling softly, and he was struck anew by how pretty she was. There was a sadness about her, though, and he wondered what her story was. For some reason, he suspected her visit to Dulcie wasn't just a catch-up with a friend.

Carla glanced up from her phone and saw him enter the cafe. When her smile widened into a beam, Ashton was gut-punched. Seeing it did something strange to his insides, and his heart stuttered.

What the hell was all that about?

Gathering himself, he made his way to her table, reining in his shock – he hadn't had such a reaction to a woman in a long time, and it wasn't welcome. He was barely out of a relationship, and now he was lusting after a woman who would be out of his life before he knew it. Or was that the attraction? Whatever it was, he had no intention of doing anything about it. It would soon pass. And even if he did want to pursue it, he highly doubted Carla would be interested.

'Hi. Ready?' he asked.

'Would you like a coffee or something before we go?'

'I'm fine.'

'Okay, then.' She picked up her bag and got to her feet. Out of the corner of his eye, he caught her biting her lip and he hoped he hadn't been too brusque.

'Do you know what camera you want?' he asked as they walked towards the shop.

'Not a clue.'

'What sort of things do you intend to photograph?'

'I'm not sure yet. Anything that catches my eye, I think.' She slowed and pointed to the cornice on one of the buildings. 'Like that, maybe. Or those.' This time, she was looking at an elderly couple who had paused outside a jewellery shop. Their hands were tightly clasped as they peered through the window, and the woman's lined face glowed when she turned her face towards her companion.

Carla asked, 'Apart from the ones you took around the farm, do you only take photos of wildlife?'

'I do photograph other things, but my favourite is wildlife in a more urban setting. Like a fox on a high street, or birds nesting in a warehouse. Here we are.' He stopped outside the shop and pushed the door, holding it open for her to enter first.

Barney looked surprised. 'Back again?'

She told Ashton, 'I was in here earlier checking out the cameras.' She turned to Barney. 'I bumped into Ashton, and he volunteered to help me choose.'

Barney nodded. 'Ashton will see you right. I'm here if you need me.'

Ashton was rather nervous at the weight of the responsibility. He wanted Carla to have the best camera she could afford but he didn't like to ask what her budget was, so he decided to start with the perfectly acceptable second-hand ones and go from there.

'This is a good one,' he said. The camera was little more than a body, but she didn't need a plethora of lenses to begin her photography journey. A couple of basic ones would do for the time being, and she could add to them later if she wished.

Twenty minutes later, they were leaving the shop, Carla clutching her purchases. She looked both eager, nervous, and slightly shell-shocked. He had to admit he was, too. She hadn't given him any indication yesterday that she intended to buy a camera, and he wondered whether she'd thought her purchase through or whether it had been an impulse buy.

'That's the hard part done,' she joked. 'Now all I have to do is learn how to use it.'

'You'll soon get the hang of it. Trial and error are the best teachers. Point, shoot, make a note of the settings, review the results.'

'I'll have to do some genning up.' Her eagerness was slipping away, and nervousness was gaining the upper hand.

'Would you like a couple of lessons?' he offered.

'Lessons?' Her eyes widened.

'Not formal ones. Just me, you, and our cameras.'

The smile was back. 'Yes, please.'

'Sunday?'

'Brilliant. Thank you so much.'

After arranging to pop up to the farm at ten o'clock on Sunday, Ashton said goodbye, and as he headed home he found he was looking forward to it. It would be nice to have some company, and he couldn't wait to see the photos she would take.

He ignored the growing suspicion that it was Carla herself that he couldn't wait to see.

CHAPTER SIX

Carla held her breath as she pressed the shutter button, then she checked the LCD and silently showed Ashton the screen. He had taken the same shot and he showed her his in return.

They weren't too dissimilar. Pleased, Carla grinned at him.

She and Ashton had been out on the hillside above the farm for the past couple of hours, taking pictures of the gorgeous scenery. Ashton had shown her how light and composition affected the outcome of an image, and she'd learnt a great deal already. But she had a feeling there was still a great deal more to learn.

She was so grateful to Ashton for accompanying her to the shop yesterday and helping her choose, because the number of cameras on display had been overwhelming. If she had been on her own, she would have probably been too confused to buy anything. Right now, she was having so much fun that she was glad she'd bought one, even if the purchase had been impulsive and not very wise under the circumstances.

The abrupt trilling of her phone shattered the peace, and Carla winced. She looked at the screen. It was Dulcie, and she wondered what she wanted. 'Sorry, I won't be a minute,' she said.

'No worries.' Ashton moved away to give her some privacy. His retreating back was broad-shouldered and slim-hipped, and as she answered the call, her eyes wandered south to his backside. Realising she was ogling him, she snatched her gaze away.

'Dulcie? What's up?'

'I've just had a thought.'

'Ooh, that's scary.'

'You're not as funny as you think you are, you know.' Dulcie's voice held a smile. 'Why don't you ask Ashton if he'd like to join us for lunch? I didn't think to mention it before you went out. I can give him his voucher at the same time.'

'Hang on. Ashton,' she called. 'Would you like to have lunch at the farm? I hear Otto does a mean Sunday roast.'

Ashton looked surprised. 'Um, that's kind, but I don't want to intrude.'

Dulcie yelled down the phone, 'Tell him he won't be!'

'Dulcie says you won't be, but if you've got other plans...?'

'My plan was a frozen pizza.'

'Tell him we're having beef with all the trimmings,' Dulcie said. 'Oh, poop, he's not vegetarian, is he?'

Carla didn't know. 'Are you a vegetarian?'

'No.'

'In that case, you're coming to lunch,' Carla told him. 'He's coming to lunch, Dulcie.'

'Great. I'll set another place. Forty-five minutes?'

'Fab.' Carla ended the call. 'We'd better get going.'

'Okay. Are you sure you don't mind?'

She gave him a sly look. 'Not at all. It means more time for lessons – unless you have to shoot off afterwards.'

When he informed her that he didn't, Carla was rather more pleased than the news warranted.

Aside from Ashton himself, there was Carla, Dulcie and Otto, Maisie and her fella Adam, as well as Beth (the girls' mother), Walter (who was Otto's dad and Beth's partner) and another sister, Nikki, plus her son Sammy, who appeared to be about twelve or thirteen. Ashton felt a little overwhelmed.

'No Gio today?' Beth asked.

Nikki shook her head. 'He's working.' She turned to Ashton. 'He's a copper.'

'I know him. He can usually be seen in a Panda car,' Ashton said.

'That's the guy,' Nikki confirmed. She and her sisters all had the same fair hair, blue eyes, and high cheekbones. They followed Beth in looks. Carla's dark hair and hazel eyes were a direct contrast, and his gaze kept drifting towards her.

Now and again, it also drifted towards Otto, and Ashton hoped the chef hadn't witnessed his debacle on the night he'd proposed to Lacey. The evening was a bit of a blur, but he could remember the way everyone in the restaurant had fallen silent as they waited for Lacey to say yes, and how the silence had stretched out uncomfortably when it became clear she wasn't going to.

Feeling overwhelmed, Ashton hung back, letting the conversation flow around him as he was invited to take a seat at the dining table.

'Before we start,' Dulcie said when everyone was seated. 'I want to give

Ashton something.' She held out a small envelope.

'What is it?' he asked.

'Open it and see.'

He prised the flap open and sucked in a breath. 'What's this for?'

'Because you refused payment, and you deserve something for your time and expertise.'

'This is too much.'

'No,' Dulcie replied, her voice firm. 'It's not.'

'I don't know what to say.' He knew he was blushing, and he felt rather embarrassed.

'No need to say anything,' Otto told him. 'Right, tuck in before it gets cold.'

Relieved that everyone's attention turned to the food, Ashton slid the gift card into the back pocket of his jeans. When he saw Carla smirk, he understood why she had been in InFocus previously the day she'd bought her camera. He narrowed his eyes at her and shook his head in admonishment.

Her smirk grew wider, and his gaze was drawn to her lips. A sudden urge to kiss them took him by surprise, and he swiftly turned his attention to his plate and tried to think about something else.

'How's business?' Otto asked Adam, handing a platter of beef to Beth, who took a couple of slices of meat and passed it on.

'Ticking along. I've got more work than I can handle to be honest, although things will calm down once the house is completed.'

'When will that be?' Walter asked. 'Last time I was up your way, it looked almost done.'

Carla leant towards Ashton and murmured, 'Adam and Maisie have a place somewhere on the mountain. He runs a machinery repair business, and Maisie is opening a kennels. They've got some building work going on.'

Adam said, 'I reckon another week or so should do it. It won't be perfect, but it'll be habitable, so if that's okay with you Beth, we'll be moving out of the house in Picklewick shortly. It'll be better if we're on site.'

Carla offered Ashton another explanation. 'The house was a shell, so he and Maisie have been living in Beth's house in Picklewick while they do it up, because she's moved in with Walter. It's a bit like musical chairs but with houses and no music.'

Ashton had noticed. The names and addresses on letters were a giveaway, and he recalled that at one time Otto used to live in the cottage on the lane with his dad, before moving into the farmhouse with Dulcie. The musical chairs analogy was quite apt.

Beth cried, 'That's earlier than you expected. How exciting!' She turned to Carla. 'Have you been up to The Forever Home yet?'

'The what?'

'Adam and Maisie's place. That's what they've called it.'

Maisie said, 'You must! It's coming along a treat. I've got some photos of the way it looked before we started work on it.'

At the mention of photos, Carla sent Ashton a warm look, and he felt a corresponding glow in his chest. The Fairfaxes and the Yorks were a close-knit family, and he was acutely conscious that he was an outsider. Perhaps Carla also felt a little like that, he mused. They were two outsiders together (despite Carla's friendship with Dulcie) with the common bond of a love of photography to bind them together, however briefly. It suddenly struck him that he didn't know how long Carla would be staying at the farm. In fact, he knew hardly anything about her, and he realised he wanted to know more.

After the best Sunday lunch Ashton had ever eaten, he and Carla went outside to resume her lesson. Despite being secretly relieved, he felt rather guilty that his offer to help with the washing up had been turned down. Clearing up after all those people was a daunting prospect. Equally daunting was the thought of asking Carla about herself, and he didn't know why he wanted to know – he just did.

'So,' he began, as they perched on bales in the barn for Carla to practice taking shots in low-level light. 'How long will you be in Picklewick?'

Her expression clouded, and he wished he hadn't asked. 'Forever, if I have my way,' she said with a sigh.

'It is beautiful up here,' he agreed, but he had a feeling the scenery wasn't the sole reason for her reluctance to leave. 'I wouldn't want to go back to Birmingham after seeing this. Not that there's anything wrong with the city,' he added hastily, 'and I'm sure it's got some lovely parks and open spaces, but...' He trailed off, not wanting to dig his hole any deeper.

She sighed. 'It's complicated.'

Ah, he thought, his spirits sinking. That sounded like man trouble.

Placing her camera on the straw, she gazed at the rafters. 'I've got a thing going on at work, a not very nice thing, and I'm on extended leave. I suppose you could say I'm hiding out here and trying to forget about it. I'll have to go home at some point, of course, and I can't impose on Dulcie for much longer, but at the moment I'm happy to be her goat walker and general dogsbody. She's trying to get me to take it easy, but I'm not really cut out for relaxing. So, in answer to your question, I honestly don't know how long I'll be here. A few more days, a week. Who knows?'

Ashton was pleased she would be here for a while longer, yet rather deflated she had to go at all, as he'd found himself enjoying her company. She was funny and smart, and her eagerness to learn was a refreshing change to the complete disinterest Lacey had shown for his hobby. He appreciated that couples didn't often like the same things, and he hadn't expected her to pick up a camera and start snapping away. But her indifference had stung, especially since he'd always shown an interest in whatever she was doing.

He should have realised they weren't compatible, but he'd been in love, and love, as the saying goes, is blind.

Ashton felt a pang when he thought of his ex, and sadness swept over him. If only Lacey could have been a little more like Carla, maybe they would have still been together.

Was there a name for when you think of something and then that very thing happens, Carla wondered, as the loud beep of an incoming message made her jump. She checked the screen and saw Vicky's name flash up, followed by the message, **I've got news!!! Call me!!!**

Carla gasped. Surely she couldn't have had the baby already? If so, the little mite was about four weeks early.

'Do you mind if I make a quick call?' she said to Ashton, realising this was the second time today she'd been contacted whilst out shooting photos with him. At least he'd gotten a nice lunch as a result of the first one. The only thing he would get out of this call would be boredom.

'Go ahead.'

He made to rise from his bale, but she waved him back down. 'It's my friend, Vicky. She's pregnant and says she's got news, so if you don't mind loads of squealing, you're welcome to stay put. I'll only be a minute, just to get the bare bones, then I'll ring her later and have a proper chat.'

Vicky sounded breathless when she answered the phone.

Carla begged, 'Please don't tell me you're in labour.'

'**What?** God, no. Is that what you thought? My bump is still here.'

'What's the news, then?'

'You remember me telling you that I was going on a training course – though why they wanted to send me on it when I'll be on maternity leave for the next six months, I don't know. Anyway,' she took a breath. 'I met someone on the course who works in the Leeds office, where Yale transferred from. Guess what she told me?'

'I've no idea.'

'She asked whether I knew him, and when I told her that he's my line manager, she wanted to know whether he was up to his old tricks yet. When I asked her what he meant, she said, **'sleeping with his staff.'** She didn't mean with **me** obviously, because I'm pregnant and the size of a small family hatchback, but with other women in the office. **Apparently**,' Vicky stressed the word, 'he had an affair with a girl in his department when he was there. Her name was Anita Campbell, and she was more into him than he was into her. She ended up resigning from her job. The woman I spoke to wasn't a hundred per cent sure what happened, but from what she could gather, he'd made life really difficult for Anita, wanting to transfer her to another department. So she left.'

Carla was silent as she absorbed the news.

Vicky said, 'Can't you see? He's got a track record.'

'But does he though? It's not a crime to have a relationship with someone you work with, even if the company frowns on it.'

'The woman reckons it was tantamount to constructive dismissal and that he was trying to distance himself from Anita because he was worried his girlfriend would find out.'

That sounded more promising. 'But it's still my word against his, and don't forget, his fiancée was a witness.'

'She only saw and heard what Yale wanted her to see and hear, and you could argue that as he's done this before, maybe his word shouldn't be taken at face value.'

'I dunno...'

'Do you want to keep your job?' Vicky demanded.

'Yes.'

'Well, then. But even if you didn't, you'll want a good reference.'

'There is that,' Carla agreed. 'It's all hearsay, though.'

'Speak to her.' Vicky urged.

'The woman on the course?'

'No, **Anita**. I've got her mobile number if you want it.'

'Um...'

'Look, I'll send it to you anyway. I haven't spoken to her myself, but the woman on the course has, so she's expecting your call. Think about it, yeah?'

'I will,' Carla promised.

After saying goodbye, the call ended, leaving her feeling dazed and confused. What should she do? Should she phone this Anita person? Or would she end up digging herself an even deeper hole?

Ashton cleared his throat.

'Oh, hell,' she muttered. She had forgotten he was there. 'How much of that did you hear?'

'Not much.'

She shot him a glance out of the corner of her eye. He was staring straight ahead.

'Okay, quite a bit,' he admitted.

'Yeah, I was afraid of that.'

'Do you want to talk about it or forget I was here?'

'Forget—' she began then paused. 'No, actually I'd like to talk about it.' Inhaling deeply, she blew out her cheeks. 'My line manager is called Yale, and we were dating for a few weeks but were keeping it quiet because the company we work for doesn't approve of line managers having romantic relationships with their staff, for obvious reasons. Anyway, one evening we went to this retirement bash and sneaked away for a quick kiss, and his fiancée caught us. Before you say anything, I had no idea he was engaged or seeing anyone else. He accused me of harassment and reported me to HR. I'm now on indefinite leave while they conduct an investigation.'

Ashton shook his head slowly. 'That's awful. I'm so sorry.'

'The thing is, Vicky says he's done something similar before,' she said, then went on to explain, ending with, 'I don't know whether I should contact this woman. Would it do any good?'

'Would it do any harm?'

'I don't know.'

'On the other hand, might it be of any use?'

'I don't know,' she repeated.

'From where I'm sitting, I don't think you've got anything to lose. But you're the one who has to make the decision and deal with whatever you discover.'

'I'll call her,' she said. Ashton was right, she didn't have anything to lose and possibly everything to gain. 'But not right now,' she added. 'I want to take some more photos.'

And neither did she want to waste any more of Ashton's time. She would contact Anita Campbell tomorrow, because she intended to enjoy the rest of the day.

The Black Horse was a typical village pub with horse brasses on the walls, beamed ceilings, and a landlord who seemed to know everyone by name.

Ashton had stepped through its doors many times, always with a letter or two in his hand and sometimes a parcel. However, he'd never visited the place for a drink, so this evening broke the trend.

After a very successful afternoon of photographing everything and anything on the hillside above the farm and in the fields around, he and Carla had made their way down the lane and into the village. And now they were sitting in the pub, examining each other's photos and contemplating an early supper. Ashton hadn't thought he would be hungry after the delicious Sunday lunch, but he had surprised himself, and was now rather peckish. He didn't want anything heavy, but a light snack would be most welcome.

Having ordered, they settled down with their drinks. 'Tell me about yourself,' he suggested.

Carla grimaced. 'Don't you know enough?'

'That's not you; that's something a turd of a bloke has done to you.' He saw her digesting this nugget of useless advice and cringed at how trite he sounded.

'I like that' she said. 'It's true.' She took a sip of her wine. 'What do you want to know?'

'How long have you and Dulcie been friends?'

'I've known her forever,' she began, and that was the start of him getting to know Carla Mason. In turn, he answered her questions, and by the time they'd eaten their meal, he felt he was beginning to understand her better.

'I've had a great day,' she said as they set off along Picklewick's main street, back towards the farm.

'So have I. We must do this again.' Even as the words left his mouth, Ashton guessed it was unlikely to happen. She could be gone tomorrow if she spoke to this Anita woman and decided her story was worth investigating.

'I'd like that. Perhaps you could show me the canal? And maybe we could have a bite to eat afterwards.'

If any other woman had made that suggestion, he would have assumed they were suggesting a date. But this was Carla, so he didn't, and he had no qualms agreeing as he said, 'We'll spot more wildlife early in the morning, rather than later in the day.'

'How early is early?'

'Five a.m.' He chuckled as her face blanched. 'Patience, the ability to stay still and quiet, and unsociable hours are often the minimum requirements for photographing wildlife.'

'Yeah, but five in the morning?' she protested.

'I'm usually up way before then,' he reminded her, 'So it's second nature to get up early on my days off.'

'Don't you ever have a lie in?'

'That's what cold and rainy winter mornings are for.'

'I wholeheartedly agree! There's nothing nicer than snuggling under the duvet when it's pitch black and belting down outside.'

Ashton had a vision of Carly's dark hair on his pillow, and he coughed. Where had **that** come from? It wasn't an unpleasant image, but it was hardly appropriate.

The image refused to go away though, lingering in the back of his mind as they negotiated Muddypuddle Lane, and he was more conscious of her than ever. He could feel the heat of her skin as her bare arm brushed against his, and he was acutely aware of the light floral scent she wore and the way the evening sun illuminated the shine of her hair.

Ashton didn't need this reaction to her, but he couldn't seem to prevent it. Thankfully, she hadn't noticed, and when he realised that she was checking out her surroundings with her newly acquired photographer's eye, he smiled.

'Ooh, toadstools!' she cried, veering to the side of the lane and crouching down to peer into the hedgerow.

Ashton followed her and lowered himself onto his haunches. The fungi were beige-brown in colour, quite tall, and the shape reminded him of a witch's hat.

'Do you know what they are?' she asked.

'Afraid not. My speciality is animals.'

'I wonder if they're edible.' She stretched out a hand.

'Don't you dare!' he cried, nudging her aside.

Unbalanced, Carla wobbled and began to topple, but before she connected with the ground Ashton's arm shot out and he grabbed her around the waist. Her momentum nearly took him down, and he pulled her towards him. Then his legs gave way, his backside plonked onto the tarmac, with the result that Carla was now sitting in his lap.

Sorry.' Ashton was mortified. 'I didn't mean to—' He stalled. Her mouth was perilously close to his, and he had the strongest urge to kiss it.

His brain disconnected from his body as his gaze focused on her lips, pink and luscious as they parted to reveal her teeth. And when she ran her tongue over her bottom lip, he found himself leaning towards her, his heart hammering and every nerve ending tingling.

Without conscious thought, his eyelids drifted shut and their lips met, sending a bolt of desire through him. Then she was kissing him back, urgently, frantically, and he wrapped both arms around her, drawing her tight against him.

God, she felt so **good.**

His reaction was unmissable and instantaneous, and he let out a groan.

A blast of a car horn cruelly broke their connection, and Ashton dragged his mouth away. Looking around, he saw a hulking big truck slowing to a halt in the middle of the lane.

He leapt to his feet and held out a hand to Carla, who looked mortified. He guessed he did, too. He certainly felt it.

When he noticed who was behind the wheel, he groaned. Trust it to be someone he knew and not a random delivery driver.

Adam was grinning down at them.

Shamefaced, Ashton scooted into the side, almost burying himself in the hedge as he did so, wishing it would swallow him whole.

The truck's window glided down. 'Want a lift?'

It was Carla who answered. 'No thanks, we're fine.'

Laughter billowed out of the cab. 'I can see that. Don't do anything I wouldn't.'

Ashton began, 'We were— It's not what—' But it was too late. Adam was revving the engine and he tooted the horn as he drove past.

Ashton waited until the truck had rounded the bend and was out of sight, then said, 'I'm sorry, I shouldn't have—'

'Don't.' Carla's voice was strangled.

He winced. **Way to go, Ashton**, he thought sourly.

'I'm not,' she said.

'Pardon?'

'I'm not sorry.'

'You aren't?'

She shook her head.

'Actually, I'm not sorry, either.' He was shocked to discover it was true. He should be, but he wasn't. The kiss had been freaking marvellous, and he desperately wanted to do it again, but he held himself in check and they walked the rest of the way in silence.

When they reached the farm, Ashton asked, 'Will I see you again?'

'I hope so.'

'When?'

'Up to you.'

'Tomorrow?'

'Yes, tomorrow.'

'It's a date,' he said, and her face broke out into a most gorgeous smile as she replied, 'Yes, I believe it is.'

CHAPTER SEVEN

Carla flinched as the hinges of the back door creaked. She had just kissed Ashton goodbye, and was now trying to sneak into the farmhouse and shuffle off to bed before Dulcie saw her face and realised something had happened.

She could hear the sound of the television coming from the living room, and assumed Dulcie and Otto were snuggled on the sofa. Which was another reason to make herself scarce. They didn't need her doing a spare wheel impression, and they deserved to spend some time alone.

Tiptoeing through the dining room and into the tiny hall, she thought she'd got away with it, but as she put her foot on the bottom step, Dulcie called out, 'Carla, is that you?'

Sheepishly, Carla stuck her head around the door, trying to use it to hide some of her face.

'Did you have a nice time?' Dulcie asked.

'Er, yeah, it was okay.'

Dulcie's gaze sharpened. 'Just okay?'

With a sigh, Carla realised she might as well come clean. Dulcie would hear about it anyway because Adam was bound to tell Maisie what he'd seen.

'We kissed,' she said, stepping into the room. Otto grinned at her.

'You didn't!' Dulcie sounded incredulous, but the disbelief was tinged with satisfaction.

Glumly, Carla replied, 'We did. In the middle of the lane.' She wrinkled her nose. 'Do you think it's possible to get high from looking at toadstools?'

'What?'

'I saw a toadstool and crouched down to have a closer look, and so did Ashton. I'm not sure what happened, but he kind of fell over, pulling me with him, and then we were kissing.'

Dulcie smirked. 'Just like that?'

'Yes, just like that. Then Adam drove up the lane and caught us.'

'He **did?** Oh, my! What happened next?'

'Nothing.'

'Nothing at all?' Dulcie's eyebrows rose.

'No. Ashton went home.'

'Are you seeing him again?'

'Yes.'

'Then why so glum?'

'For one, I don't make a habit of sitting in the middle of a road, snogging. For another, I don't want to get involved with anyone. Not here, and definitely not now.'

'So why are you seeing him again?

Carla shrugged. Admittedly, she was attracted to him and enjoyed his company, but was that sufficient reason to go on a date?

Her inner voice let out a snide laugh, and she was forced to admit that she'd gone on dates for far less valid reasons.

'A bit of fun will do you good,' Dulcie continued.

'I didn't come here for fun. I came here to cry on your shoulder, not to get involved with some guy.'

'But you like him and he likes you, otherwise he wouldn't be helping you with your photography.'

There's no future in it,' Carla pointed out.

'Since when have you been bothered about the future? It's a date, not a marriage proposal.'

Carla decided to change the subject. 'I spoke to Vicky earlier,' she began and proceeded to recount the conversation, ending with, 'I'm going to call Anita Campbell in the morning.'

As Carla prepared for bed, she assumed she would lie awake mulling over the information Vicky had given her, and how, if it were true, it could affect the hearing.

However, it wasn't that which occupied her thoughts, it was Ashton – because as kisses went, it had been simply delicious.

Ashton's shift seemed to last forever. It was the longest shift he'd worked in his life, each minute feeling more like an hour, and he found himself hurrying through his round as though getting back to the depot earlier meant he could knock off earlier. It didn't, unfortunately.

He'd not had any post for the farm today and he couldn't decide whether he was disappointed, before coming down on the side of relief. He had a feeling that seeing Carla whilst he was at work might prove awkward.

But when he thought about their date later, his pulse quickened and there was a flutter in his chest, which was concerning. He was on a hiding to nothing, and he warned himself not to get carried away. Carla was gorgeous and he liked her immensely, but she would be out of his life soon, so he should enjoy this for what it was.

Unfortunately, he didn't know what it was. A confidence boost maybe? A reassurance that not every woman found him as boring as Lacey did. That he still had it, whatever it was. Actually, scrap that – he'd never been particularly popular with the girls. Too much of a nerd, he guessed. Not athletic, or edgy.

There was one thing you could say about him – his nan, bless her heart, often told him what a nice boy he was, but he suspected that was because he smuggled bottles of stout into the care home for her. His mum would have a fit if she knew.

He wondered whether he would have time to pay Nan a quick visit this morning, since he'd managed to get ahead with his round. She lived in Honeymead Care Home on the outskirts of Picklewick, which was on his round, and he tried to call in wherever he could.

Deciding he did, he popped into the off-licence in Picklewick's high street and bought her a couple of bottles and a multi-pack of spicy Nik Naks. That should see her right for a couple of days.

When he arrived at the care home, he was buzzed inside immediately and handed the stack of post to Rose on the reception desk.

'How's my grandmother today?' he asked.

'As chirpy as always. She's in the day room, waiting to have her hair done.'

Perfect. The day room took him past her bedroom, which meant he could smuggle in the bottles of stout and hide them at the back of her wardrobe behind her shoes.

He was in and out in a flash and striding into the day room with no one any the wiser.

His nan spotted him immediately, and her face lit up in a big smile. 'Ashton, my lovely boy. Come give your nana a kiss.' When he bent down to kiss her cheek, she hissed in his ear, 'Did you bring me any stout?'

'It's in the usual place.'

'You're a good boy.'

'I haven't got long,' he warned, sitting in the chair next to her.

'I guessed as much.' She fingered the sleeve of his Royal Mail tee shirt. 'How are you?'

'I'm good.' Her eyes narrowed, and she gave him a beady stare before her expression softened. 'You look better than the last time I saw you. Not as sad.' She pulled a face. 'I never did like Lacey. She didn't have any taste.'

'Because she turned me down?' He gave his grandmother a rueful smile.

'Partly. And because she thought her poop didn't smell.'

'Nan! That's not nice.'

'It's true,' his grandmother said. 'She thought she was too good for you.' A fierce light shone in her eyes. 'No one is good enough for my grandson.'

'You're biased.'

'I'm right. Now, what's your news?'

'I haven't got any.'

'Liar. I can see it in your face.'

Thankfully Ashton was saved from further questioning when his nan's attention was caught by one of the carers gesturing to her.

'It's my turn.' His nan patted her hair. 'I was thinking of having it coloured pink.'

'Go for it, Nan.'

'That's what I love about you,' she said, pinching his cheek as he helped her get to her feet and find her walking stick. 'Nothing ever rattles you. Not even that Lacey business. Right, I'm off for my pampering session. I was only joking about the colour, by the way.'

Ashton watched her shuffle down the corridor, his heart full of love, and as he left the care home, he idly wondered whether she would also think that Carla wasn't good enough for him.

The Golden Fleece in Thornbury was a trendy bar. Not really his scene (he preferred quieter, more traditional watering holes) but Ashton thought Carla might enjoy it. The food was supposed to be good, and the selection of gins was astounding. Not that he would sample any, as he couldn't stand the stuff, but he hoped Carla liked them.

He had collected her from the farm, conscious of a shadowy figure peering out of the kitchen window, and guessed it was Dulcie. There was an awkward moment when he wondered whether Carla expected a kiss, before they settled for a peck on the cheek and a brief hug.

And now they were sitting in the bar across the table from one another, debating whether to have a starter. He had the feeling Carla seemed reluctant, and guessed she might be worried about the price of the meal. This place wasn't cheap, although it wasn't as expensive as The Wild Side.

As though she'd read his mind, Carla said, 'Otto suggested we dine at The Wild Side, rather than drag you all the way to Picklewick to pick me up, then drive all the way here. I know Thornbury's not far, but...'

Ashton's mouth tightened and his jaw clenched. The Wild Side was the last place he wanted to eat at.

He thought he'd covered his reaction, but he clearly hadn't, as Carla said, 'I know it's pricey, but Otto wouldn't charge us the full amount.'

'It's not that—'

'Please don't tell me you've had a bad experience there,' she interrupted, then saw his expression. 'Oh, dear, you have.'

'Not in the way you think. The food was lovely, the occasion not so much.'

She was looking at him expectantly, and he realised he couldn't leave it there. He had to give her an explanation. He took a steadying breath. 'I proposed to my girlfriend there. She turned me down.'

Carla's expression was full of sympathy. 'It seems neither of us has been lucky in love.' She paused, and he could see her thinking. 'The Wild Side hasn't been open very long, so I assume this was fairly recent?'

'It was.' He drank some of his sparkling water, the pain of Lacey's rejection hitting him anew.

Carla said, 'I'm sorry.'

'I'll get over it.' He stared into space, his smile sad. 'It was probably for the best. We weren't compatible. Wanted different things out of life. And she didn't approve of my hobby. Said it was boring.' Then he added, 'She said I was boring, and that I lacked ambition.' He grimaced. 'She's right, I do, and I'm not going to apologise.'

'I don't think you're boring.'

'That's kind of you.'

'I'm being honest. I think you're fascinating.' Her eyes widened. 'I mean, photography is fascinating and you're a photographer, so...'

He chuckled. 'I know what you mean. But I'm the first to admit that I'm not the most exciting person in the world. I'm a postman, for goodness' sake, and I like my job. I don't want promotion or more responsibility.'

She giggled. 'I bet I can beat you in a 'who is the most boring' contest. I work in insurance for a start, and I still live at home.'

Oh, that's definitely a point for you. At least I've got my own place,' he teased.

'In my defence, my mum works for a travel company as a rep and she's away for months on end, so it's almost as good as having my own house, but without the mortgage.'

'No mortgage,' he said dreamily. 'I can't imagine what that's like.'

'I keep thinking I should move out and put a toe on the property ladder, but I can't afford it unless I do a flat-share thing, and I don't fancy that. I like my own space.'

'What would happen if your mum came back for good?'

'I'd have to move out, I think. The thought of bringing someone back when she's there...' Carla shuddered, then bit her lip. 'Not that I take men home very often.'

'You don't have to explain or justify anything.'

'But I don't want you to think—'

'I don't.' He hoped she could hear the sincerity in his voice. 'Shall we order? We've been nursing these menus for ages, and the waiter is hovering.'

With their orders given, Ashton remembered to ask her whether she had phoned Anita-what's-her-face today.

'I did,' Carla replied with a frown. 'But she wasn't prepared to discuss it over the phone. She wants to meet in person.'

'Is that a problem?'

'She might be a stalker or something. Besides, she lives in Leeds.'

'Will it help your case if you go?'

'I don't know until I talk to her. I discussed it with my union rep, and he said that depending on the information she gives me, it might help.'

'You should go.'

'I suppose.'

'Would you like me to come with you?'

Carla gasped. 'You'd do that?'

'Absolutely.'

'Why?'

'Because the guy is a jerk, and he shouldn't be allowed to get away with it. And I can see how much you're hurting.'

Her smile was warm. 'Has anyone told you that you're a very nice man?'

Ashton didn't say anything, and if Carla had been aware of the lustful thoughts that went through his mind when he kissed her good night later, she would have quickly changed her opinion of him.

Carla was seriously cheesed off that HR hadn't been in touch with her regarding a date for the meeting. How much longer was this going to go on? She was in limbo until it was resolved.

The silver lining, as Ashton pointed out on the journey to Leeds, was that at least the delay had given her time to speak to Anita Campbell.

Ashton, she'd discovered, usually looked on the bright side and his cheerfulness was rubbing off on her. In his company, she couldn't be morose. She was so glad he'd offered to accompany her today, and not just because it saved her from an arduous train journey. If it hadn't been for him, Carla might have been tempted to return to Birmingham and stay there, rather than travel back and forth to Picklewick, because she was conscious of not outstaying her welcome at the farm.

As soon as she returned to Muddypuddle Lane this evening, she really should have a discussion with Dulcie, because she honestly didn't know how long this situation would continue. It could be a matter of days, or weeks. God forbid, it might even be months, and there was no way she could stay with Dulcie for that length of time, no matter how useful she tried to be.

Unfortunately, Carla didn't want to return to Birmingham. She was quite settled at the farm, and neither did she want to leave Ashton. She would miss him more than was wise.

Over the past few days she had developed feelings for him, and that didn't sit well with her. She had got over Yale far too quickly for comfort (despite how he'd treated her), so what did that say about her?

Carla feared she couldn't trust herself to know how she felt anymore. Gone was the carefree woman who had been happy to have fun and not allow any man to touch her heart, and Carla missed her. She'd known where she was with that version of herself. She'd vaguely recognised the version who had thought she'd fallen in love with Yale, but this more sombre, serious Carla, who had developed a sneaking enjoyment of the countryside and a love of photography, was a complete stranger.

And she hadn't even begun to pick apart her growing feelings for Ashton.

She couldn't think about that now though, because they were nearing the outskirts of Leeds and heading for a place called Morley, just off the M62. After negotiating a tangled mess of a junction, Carla was glad to leave the motorway behind.

'Not far now,' Ashton said. The car's satnav was a godsend, and within a few minutes it had directed them to their destination.

Carla levered her stiff body out of the car. 'That was one hell of a journey. This had better be worth it. If Anita Campbell has led us on a wild goose chase, I won't be responsible for my actions.'

'I think I've aged ten years,' Ashton groaned. 'When I looked up the route online, it reckoned it should take around three and a half hours, not five. Thank goodness we set out in plenty of time, otherwise we would be late. I'm not looking forward to the drive back.'

'I bet you're wishing you hadn't offered.'

He looked her in the eye. 'Not at all.'

She met his gaze and held it, feeling a shiver travel down her back. Then she looked away. She'd unpick that later; right now, she needed to focus.

They were twenty minutes early, so Carla didn't expect Anita to be there yet. After making enquiries with a member of staff in the pub where they'd agreed to meet, Carla was directed to a table. A woman was already seated there, a glass of what looked like orange juice in front of her, alongside a cardboard document wallet.

Carla took a moment to study her. She was a pretty redhead, with curling locks, freckles, and the most gorgeous green eyes. Nothing like Carla, or Yale's fiancée. It appeared the man didn't have a type, unless **gullible** could be called a type.

'Anita?' Carla asked hesitantly.

'You must be Carla.' Anita gave Ashton a doubtful look, as though she hadn't expected Carla to have brought anyone with her.

'This is Ashton. He drove me here.'

Anita indicated they should sit, and once they were settled she pushed the document wallet across the table. 'This is why I wanted to speak to you in person,' she said.

'What is it?' Carla opened the envelope flap and slid out a sheaf of papers.

'Messages between me and Yale.' Anita spat out his name. 'He denied he sent them, and he even deleted his side of the conversation so there would be no record. But I'd taken screenshots.'

Carla was perplexed. 'Why did you do that?'

'I had a stalker a few years ago, and now I always screenshot anything that can disappear, just in case.' Her tone was matter-of-fact.

Carla flicked through them, scanning them quickly. Oh, my...

Anita said, 'I could have emailed them to you, but I wanted to meet you in person. I can't believe he did it again. I heard he took it further and reported you to HR. What a snake.'

Carla told her the full story, and Anita nodded along. When she'd finished speaking, Anita asked, 'What does his fiancée look like?'

'Tall, thin, dressed to the nines, with bouncy blonde hair. Expensive looking.'

'That's the woman he cheated on when he was with me, but she was his girlfriend then, not his fiancée. Her father is really well off. I mean, **really.** He's just started a new venture in Birmingham, something to do with luxury cars.'

'Is that why Yale transferred to the Birmingham office from Leeds?'

'I expect so.'

'He's a fool to be playing around,' Carla said.

'He's an arrogant so-and-so. I think he honestly believes he isn't going to get caught.'

'And even when he does, he comes out of it smelling of roses.' Carla was incensed.

Anita tapped the folder. 'I left the company of my own accord without a fuss, because I couldn't face the fallout.' Her eyes filled with tears. 'I loved him so much, and he broke my heart.' She blinked furiously. 'I wish I hadn't let him walk all over me. I wish I'd stayed and fought, but I didn't have it in me. Not then. I'm not sure I do now, to be honest. But I think you do.'

Carla nodded slowly. 'You're right, I do.' However, she wasn't sure whether the contents of this folder or what Anita had told her would be enough.

Anita said sombrely, 'Look at the last couple of printouts.'

Carla did. They weren't screenshots of messages and neither were they emails or photographs. They were transcripts of phone conversations. And what they said made Carla's blood boil. Yale really was a nasty piece of work.

'Are these verbatim?' she asked.

'They are.'

'You could have made all this up. I know you didn't,' she added hastily, 'but that's what they will say.'

'I expect they will, if that was all there is.' There was steel in Anita's eyes. 'I recorded both conversations. I know what he did to me isn't exactly the same as what he did to you, but it's close enough. He won't have a leg to stand on!'

Carla felt exhausted as she and Ashton returned to his car later that afternoon.

Anita had left shortly after her revelation, promising to keep in touch, so Carla and Ashton had decided to grab something to eat before tackling the long drive back to Picklewick. It had taken nearly five hours to get to Leeds, due to traffic and roadworks along several lengths of the motorways, and there was no reason to think the return journey would be any less fraught.

Carla was shattered, and she wasn't the one who would be doing the driving! Poor Ashton must be seriously regretting accompanying her today. It was a pity they couldn't break the journey—

She slapped a hand to her forehead. Of course! 'I've got an idea,' she said. 'We could come off the motorway at Birmingham and stay the night at my house.' Then she felt a fool for mentioning it, as she remembered something. 'Oh, but you can't – you've got work tomorrow.'

Ashton's smile was more of a smirk. 'Actually, I don't. I arranged to have tomorrow off because I knew today would be a long day.'

Carla was touched that he'd gone to all that trouble. 'I don't know what to say.'

'You don't have to say anything. You'd do the same for me.'

She was surprised to realise that she would. 'Does that mean you're happy to break the journey at mine?'

'I don't see why not. I must admit, I wasn't looking forward to driving back this afternoon. Anyway, I've never been to Birmingham.'

'Do you want to go out on the town this evening?' Carla hoped not. It was the last thing she was in the mood for.

'What? Not on your life! I was hoping to see an urban fox.'

Carla might have known, and she rolled her eyes good-naturedly. 'Pity you didn't bring your camera.'

'I know,' he sighed. 'I didn't think I'd need it.'

'I don't think you'll need it tonight, either. I've never seen a fox on my street.'

'Have you looked for one?'

'Not really.'

He gave her a 'well, then,' look.

She said, 'Are you sure I can't tempt you to go for a drink down my local?'

'Oh, go on then, you've twisted my arm.'

'Were you having me on about wanting to see a fox?

His face creased into a smile, his profile showing her one of his gorgeous dimples.

'Only a bit. A pie and a pint will go down a treat.'

'You've just eaten,' she pointed out.

'And I'll want to eat again before I go to bed. My job means I'm on my feet for a lot of the day.' He tapped his flat stomach. 'I need the calories.'

Carla barely heard that last bit. She'd zeroed in on the word 'bed' and it abruptly struck her that she would be alone in the house with a man she found seriously attractive and a thoroughly nice guy. And he would be sleeping in the bedroom next to hers.

Maybe, given how fast her heart was beating at the thought and how dry her mouth had suddenly become, suggesting he stayed the night at her place wasn't the best idea she'd ever had.

By the time they'd exited the motorway at Birmingham, Ashton was more than ready to ditch the car and stretch his legs. He wasn't used to sitting in one position for this long, or being so sedentary, and his back was in half. To add to his woes, his neck was stiff, his shoulders were aching, and his eyes felt gritty from focusing so hard.

The return journey had been twice as bad, with even more traffic to contend with, and he'd seen more near misses in one day than he'd witnessed in a year in Thornbury.

Carla guided him through the unfamiliar one-way system, and when she finally instructed him to pull onto a driveway outside a semi-detached 1930s house in a leafy suburb, he sighed in relief.

Ashton got out of the car, groaning as his muscles protested, and looked around. 'Is there a shop nearby?' he asked, wishing he had suggested they push on, rather than agreeing to break the journey. He wasn't exactly prepared for an overnight stay. 'I need a toothbrush.'

Carla unlocked the front door, bending down to pick up a wad of post and giving him a view of her shapely behind. He swallowed and looked away.

'There are new toothbrushes in the bathroom,' she told him, flicking through the letters and flyers. She paused, and her face paled. Then she held up an envelope sporting a logo he recognised as belonging to a large insurance company. 'It's from work,' she said. 'And it sure as hell isn't a renewal quote.'

He followed her inside, noting her automatic actions as she draped her bag over the newel post and kicked off her shoes in the hall. He wondered whether he should follow suit but became distracted by her cute bare feet with their apricot-painted toenails.

She tore the envelope open. 'Would you like a cup of tea or coffee? Blast, there won't be any fresh milk.'

'Would you like me to pop out and fetch some?' he offered, thinking she might want some time alone to read the letter.

'Only if you want tea,' she replied absently, her eyes on the letter. 'There's creamer for coffee. Or wine. I'm deffo having wine.' She blew out her cheeks and waved the letter. 'I've got a date for my meeting with HR.'

'When?'

'Two weeks Friday.' She threw it onto the worktop and opened the fridge. Ashton saw there wasn't a lot in there, but there were two bottles of red. 'The glasses are in that cupboard,' she said, jerking her chin as she unscrewed the top of one of them.

He took two out and set them down. 'Isn't it good news that you have a date?'

She gulped her wine, drinking half of it in one go. 'I'm scared.'

'I expect you are. I would be, too. The prospect of being sacked can't be pleasant, but at least you'll know one way or the other. And from what Anita said, you probably won't be sacked, but **he** might. You'll be back at your desk in no time.'

Another gulp. Her glass was nearly empty.

Then Carla's chin wobbled, and her eyes filled with tears.

Ashton put down his drink and held out his arms. He couldn't do anything about her job situation, but he could give her his moral support. A cuddle mightn't make anything better, but it certainly wouldn't make it worse.

He held her for a long time, and the longer he held her the more reluctant he was to let her go. It felt so natural, so right to have her in his arms, her cheek against his shoulder, his face in her hair, and at that moment, Ashton realised he was in danger of losing his heart.

CHAPTER EIGHT

Dulcie was in the dining room on a call with a customer when Carla walked into the farmhouse the following morning. As she headed towards the stairs, her friend beckoned her over, then held up an index finger to signify that she wouldn't be long.

Carla sank into a chair while she waited, her thoughts flicking back to last night. No doubt Dulcie would give her the Spanish Inquisition treatment as soon as she got off the phone.

Dulcie's attention was on the screen but when she'd finished speaking to the customer, she tore off her headset and swivelled around in her seat. 'Did you spend the night together?' she demanded, her face alight with curiosity.

'Yes.'

'I knew it!' Dulcie punched the air. 'I said as much to Otto after you messaged me to say you were staying at yours. Thanks for that, by the way – I'd have been worried.' She fixed Carla with a piercing look. 'Did you get much sleep?'

'Not a lot.'

'Ooh. He looks like he might be a considerate lover. Was he?'

Carla smiled sweetly. 'I've no idea.' Then she burst out laughing at Dulcie's confusion. 'We spent the night at my place,' she confirmed, 'but not in the same bed. Ashton slept in the spare room.' She giggled. 'Your face was a picture.'

'But what about the 'not a lot of sleep' thing?'

'I didn't sleep well, but that had nothing to do with Ashton,' she fibbed, as her restlessness having been mostly because of him. Some of it had been due to worry over the forthcoming meeting with HR, mulling over the contents of the folder (there had even been a photo of Yale and Anita kissing, which was pure gold) and a feeling of complete and utter dislocation from her life in Birmingham.

She had spent half the night wondering how much she would miss Picklewick (and Ashton, **especially Ashton**) and fearing she would miss it far more than was good for her. What she couldn't decide was whether her reluctance to go home to Birmingham was the result of the usual post-holiday dismay at returning to real life that most people experienced, or whether there was more to it.

As she had lain in bed last night, the room illuminated by streetlights and the subdued noise of the city in the small hours reminding her of the rumbling of a sleeping giant, she had been shocked to discover that she didn't want this anymore. When she tried to imagine herself slotting back into this house, her job, and the social scene she had previously embraced with enthusiasm, she couldn't. It felt like a well-loved dress that had been worn all the time, but had now grown shabby and no longer fitted the way it once had.

When she closed her eyes, all she could envisage was the hillside above the farm, with the wind in the grass and the cry of birds overhead. All she could feel was the weight of a camera in her hand and the peace in her soul.

Dulcie was gazing at her in concern. 'How was your meeting? Was it useful?'

'It certainly was.' Carla pulled the document wallet from her bag and passed it over.

Dulcie flicked through it. 'Bloody hell, this is dynamite!'

'It is.' She wrinkled her nose.

'Don't you think this will be enough?' Dulcie asked.

'It should be.'

'What aren't you telling me?'

'I want to be exonerated – of course I do – but I don't believe I can work there after this.'

Dulcie's mouth fell open. 'But you love your job.' She scooted her chair closer, the wheels squeaking on the polished floorboards. 'Don't let this spoil things. You'll be back at your desk in no time and in an hour it'll be as though you'd never been away.'

'That's what worries me.'

'I don't understand.'

'I'm not sure I do, either.'

'What's going on, Carla? Has something happened?'

Carla got to her feet. 'Ignore me, I'm being silly. I'll feel better after I take a goat for a walk.'

'You don't have to. I think they're lead-trained by now. Why don't you have a quiet day? Read a book or something.'

Carla shook her head. 'I'd prefer to go for a walk.' She wanted a final look around before she left.

'Something **has** happened. Tell me. Is it Ashton?'

'Real life has happened. I had a letter from HR. The meeting is almost three weeks away. I can't stay here until then.'

'Why not?'

'Because I can't.'

'You **can**,' Dulcie insisted. 'I love having you here.'

'And I love being here.'

'What will you do in Birmingham? Mope, that's what.'

Dulcie was probably right, Carla thought. Then she brightened; at least she would have her newfound love of photography to keep her occupied.

'Have you spoken to your mum about this?' Dulcie demanded.

'Not yet.'

'Give her a call, see what she says.'

It was a good idea. Taking the folder with her, Carla went to her room. Dropping wearily onto the bed and narrowly missing

Magic who was napping there, she messaged her mum. **Call me? I've got news.** It was still early in St Lucia, so hopefully she'd catch her mum before she began work.

Her phone rang a second later, and Carla felt some of the tension drain away when she heard her mother's voice.

'How are you, sweetheart? How was your trip to Leeds?'

Carla had been keeping her mum informed via messaging, but it wasn't the same as speaking to her in person. She relaxed into the pillows, the cat curling into her and Carla absently stroked its silky head.

'Interesting,' she replied and filled her mum in on everything that had happened. **Nearly** everything. Although she'd told Mum about Ashton and that he'd helped her with the camera purchase, she hadn't mentioned kissing him. Or that her feelings for him had gone beyond casual friendship. Actually, she wasn't entirely sure **what** her feelings were.

'It was weird being back home yesterday,' she said at the end of the explanation. 'It didn't feel like home anymore.'

'Good.'

'Excuse me?'

'I said, **good**. It's about time you thought about spreading your wings.'

'Are you trying to get rid of me?'

'Never. It will always be your home and you'll always be welcome, but you need your own space.'

'Hang on, Mum, I can't think about getting a place of my own when I don't know whether I'll have a job at the end of the month.'

'You will. And when all this is behind you, you can have a good think about what you want to do with your life.' There was a pause, then her mum blurted, 'I wish I could be there with you. I hate to think of you rattling around in that house on your own, miserable and lonely.'

She had a point. Carla **would** be miserable and lonely. 'Dulcie has asked me to stay on at the farm, but I don't want to intrude any more than I already have.'

'If Dulcie didn't want you, she wouldn't have suggested it.'

'True, but I do feel guilty. Everyone descends on her. Otto must be a bloody saint to put up with it.'

'I'd like to meet him. I've never met a celebrity chef.'

Carla laughed. 'Next time you're home, I'll see what I can do. But perhaps we'll stay in one of Picklewick's B & Bs rather than at the farm, otherwise Dulcie might get you cleaning out the chicken coop.'

'Ugh, no thanks! I'd better go, work calls. Let me know what you decide. Stay safe, sweetheart. I love you.'

'Love you too, Mum.'

When Carla went downstairs, Dulcie wasn't at her desk. She was in the kitchen, on her mobile phone. When she spied Carla, she ended the call and beamed at her.

'I've had a brilliant idea,' she announced.

But when Carla wanted to know what it was, Dulcie refused to say anything further.

'If you think I'm walking up this hill, you can think again,' Dulcie told Carla a short time later, as her little hatchback groaned up the rutted track behind the farm which led to the top of the mountain. Carla hadn't been up this way, preferring to take the less arduous path around the side of the hill.

'Where are we going?' she asked.

'To Adam and Maisie's place.'

'Is it far?'

'Far enough, which is why we're not on foot.'

'Where is Maisie anyway? I didn't see her at the farm.'

'That's because she isn't there. She's at The Forever Home.'

Carla didn't bother asking any more questions, since Dulcie was being evasive, and stared out of the window instead.

The top of the mountain was a wilder place than its slopes, bleaker and windswept, with bracken and long grass stretching into the distance. There was no peak as such, just rolling grassland dotted with sheep, that seemed to go on forever.

When they finally reached a cluster of buildings, Maisie hurried out and the sisters greeted each other, then Maisie gave Carla a hug.

'It's looking good, Maisie,' Dulcie said, gazing at the house.

'Want to see inside?'

'Duh! Does a sheep poop in the heather? Lead the way!' Dulcie turned to Carla. 'I haven't been up here for a few weeks, and there wasn't any plaster on the walls last time I came.'

When they stepped inside, Dulcie let out a low whistle. 'Oh, wow. I can't believe this was once a shell with no roof and a tree growing in the middle of the living room.'

Neither could Carla. Maisie and Adam's house looked like something out of a magazine, with whitewashed walls, vaulted ceilings and polished hardwood floors. It was the ultimate in barn conversions.

Maisie said to Dulcie, 'As I told you on the phone, we're moving in on the weekend, so any help will be appreciated.'

'I'm sure Carla and I can hump a few boxes around. Especially since it will be in Carla's best interests.'

Carla was bemused. 'It will?' Despite Dulcie's offer and her mum's advice, she wasn't entirely sure she would still be here at the weekend. She had to go home at some point, and the jury was still out on when that would be.

Both Dulcie and Maisie were grinning at her.

'What?' she demanded, wondering if she was missing something obvious.

Maisie repeated, 'We are moving into this house on the weekend.'

'Yes, you said.'

'Which means, I'm moving **out** of the house in Picklewick.'

'Okay...'

'It's rented. There's a couple of months left on the lease.'

It dawned on Carla what Maisie was getting at. 'I can't afford it,' she stated flatly.

'You won't have to. Adam and I aren't paying any rent. My mum is. She's the one who's supposed to be renting it. When she came to Picklewick, she took out a six-month lease but ended up moving in with Walter, as you know. Me and Adam have been living in it while we renovated this place. She said you can move into her house until you're ready to return to Birmingham.'

Carla didn't know much about property rental, but she knew enough. 'Isn't that classed as subletting?' she pointed out.

Dulcie answered, 'It is, but both the estate agent who manages the property and the landlord are okay with it.'

'Blimey.' Carla didn't know what to say. It was a generous offer, but... 'I haven't got any furniture. Not a stick to my name.'

Maisie said, 'Mum has. It's her furniture in the house at the moment. Adam's is in storage.' She pulled a face. 'Mum's stuff is really old-fashioned, so we won't be bringing any of it with us to the new place.

What do you say? Are you going to move in for the duration?'

'Yes – I think.'

To say she was shocked was an understatement, and she wasn't sure she was doing the right thing. Still, it was only for a couple of weeks, and it occurred to her that this was an opportunity to try living on her own. It would also allow her to find out what it would be like to live in Picklewick itself – because she knew, without a shadow of a doubt, that she didn't want to leave.

'We've got to stop eating out,' Carla protested as she and Ashton tucked into a sharing plate of Tex-Mex later that evening. They were dining in one of Ashton's favourite restaurants, one he didn't get to eat in often because Lacey didn't like the food.

'I know, but I thought we should mark the occasion,' he said, popping a taco in his mouth. Mmm, delicious!

'Me moving into Beth's house for a couple of weeks is hardly a cause for celebration.'

'I think it is.' He met her gaze solemnly, stretching a hand across the table to slip into hers.

It meant she wasn't leaving yet, and that was all he could think about – Carla leaving Picklewick and him never seeing her again. It was all he had been able to think about since yesterday, because seeing her in Birmingham had brought it home to him that she wouldn't be in Picklewick much longer. And it also reinforced the fact that he really didn't want her to go. A couple more weeks was definitely something to be celebrated as far as he was concerned.

She opened her mouth, then closed it again, and he wondered what she had been about to say. He considered asking but decided against it. He didn't know her well enough to pry into her thoughts. **What are you thinking**, was the kind of question lovers might ask one another. Although he wouldn't say no to taking her to bed (he was a red-blooded man with a healthy libido, after all), they weren't at that stage in their relationship and never would be. They were friends with kisses (not benefits), and he doubted they would be anything more than that. Which was a good thing, as he didn't want to fall for this woman any more than he already had.

But it didn't mean he couldn't kiss her, and he shuffled his chair around so he could do precisely that.

'Dulcie took me to see Beth's house this afternoon,' Carla said as they broke apart, the kiss too fleeting for his liking. 'It's perfect. You'll have to visit. I move in on Saturday.'

'I will,' he promised.

'What's your place like?'

'Small.'

'One bed or two?'

'Two, but the spare room is mostly filled with camera equipment.' Which reminded him – he hadn't yet spent the voucher Dulcie had given him. Maybe he would get Carla a new lens? It could be her going away present.

Shrugging off the thought of her leaving, he said, 'You'll have to pop over and see it. My camera stuff, I mean. Not the house. The house is nothing special.'

'At least it's yours,' she countered.

'There is that,' he agreed.

'And you promised to show me the canal.'

'So I did. Would you like to go on Sunday? I warn you, it'll be an early start.' He paused. 'Or will you be too busy unpacking?'

'I've got one suitcase. It's not going to take long.'

'Do you think you'll like living in Picklewick?'

She considered the question. 'I'm not sure. I love being at the farm, but I'm kind of in holiday mode at the moment. It's going to be a big jump to move from Birmingham to a little village. I'm worried it might be too sedate, if that's the right word.'

He laughed. 'I'm sure you'll be able to manage being sedate for a couple of weeks.'

'Yeah, I'm sure I will.' She laughed too, but it sounded strained, and he wondered whether she regretted her decision not to return to Birmingham immediately.

As he tried to figure it out, he felt a prickling on the back of his neck and glanced over his shoulder to see a familiar face staring at him. His heart sank. This was the last place he expected to see Lacey, considering she didn't like the food.

Her gaze drilled into him, and he squirmed uncomfortably. She was with one of her friends, and he couldn't help thinking how this must look, him being here with another woman barely two months since he'd proposed.

Ashton managed to tear his gaze away, and as he caught a waiter's eye, he tried to make it appear as though that was what he'd intended all along. 'Could we have some water for the table, please?'

'So, the canal,' Carla was saying, oblivious. 'Is it far from your house?'

'Nothing in Thornbury is far from anywhere else,' he joked weakly. 'It's bigger than Picklewick, but it's not city sized.'

'It's got everything you need though, right?'

'I suppose.' He could still feel the weight of Lacey's stare. She must think that he'd either got over her very quickly or Carla was a rebound relationship.

He swallowed hard and risked another glance. This was the first time he'd set eyes on her since he'd proposed. He'd phoned and he'd messaged, to no avail. She hadn't answered his calls or returned his messages, yet now there was a jealous expression on her face that had no right to be there.

Then it occurred to him that her expression mightn't have anything to do with him, and he scolded himself for thinking the world revolved around him. Clearly her world hadn't, because if it had, she wouldn't have dumped him. Right now, she was probably thinking he was a sad fecker and that she'd had a lucky escape. Maybe she was even feeling sorry for Carla.

Ashton had no appetite for dessert and was eager to leave. Despite it being early still, Carla didn't appear to want to linger either. They had been in the restaurant for one hour and fifteen minutes, tops. Some date this was turning out to be.

'Fancy a walk?' he asked impulsively. 'I thought we could stroll along the towpath.'

Carla glanced at her feet. 'I'm not really dressed for it.'

He followed the direction of her gaze. She was wearing strappy sandals with heels, so there was nothing for it but to take her home, unless... 'Want to pop back to my place?' he asked, as they made towards the car.

She was smiling. 'For coffee?

'If you want, or I can open a bottle of wine.'

She raised her eyebrows and tilted her head. 'You really do mean coffee.'

'Why? What did you—? **Oh.**'

'You're blushing.'

'I'm not.'

'It's cute.'

'Cute?' He didn't want to be thought of as cute. He wanted to be thought of as rugged and handsome. 'I withdraw my offer,' he joked.

'Please don't. I want to see your equipment.' Realising what she'd said, she closed her eyes and let out a groan.

Her blush made him chuckle. 'You've gone red.' He was laughing aloud now, a proper belly laugh that left him gasping for breath. Carla glared at him for a moment before giggling, and very soon she had tears in her eyes and was holding her sides.

'I haven't laughed like that for ages,' she gasped.

And when he replied, 'I'm glad the thought of seeing my equipment amuses you,' it set her off again.

She leaned against him for support, and he slipped an arm around her waist. When she straightened up, it was perfectly natural for his mouth to seek hers and he simply didn't care that they were snogging in the street like teenagers.

When they broke apart, Ashton was breathless with desire.

'I think I'll have that glass of wine you mentioned,' she said.

He took hold of her hand, and they resumed their walk to the car.

'After **coffee**,' she added, leaning in to nibble on his ear.

Ashton stumbled, as what she said sank in; did she mean what he **thought** she meant?

The short journey from the restaurant to his house seemed to take forever. The tension between them was palpable, and the atmosphere in the car was charged with promise.

Ashton's pulse throbbed, his palms were clammy on the steering wheel, and his thoughts were a confused mess. He wanted her so badly it hurt, but was what they were about to do wise?

Sod it.

He was going into this with his eyes wide open. He knew what he was letting himself in for – a relationship with Carla would never be a long-term thing – and as long as he kept that in mind, he should be fine.

Carla pushed her misgivings aside as desire surged through her veins. Ashton's smouldering look when he'd realised what she'd meant, and the way his eyes had darkened, the tension in his jaw and the hunger on his face, had melted her insides, searing its way through her body.

Dear lord, she hadn't felt this turned on since forever. And he hadn't even touched her yet. Not really – although the kiss they'd just shared had nearly made her burst into flames.

By the time they arrived at his house, her heart was skipping, missing beats and thudding to catch up with itself, and she was so weak with desire that she had trouble getting out of the car.

As soon as they were inside, he turned to her and she swallowed reflexively, wilting at the naked desire in his eyes.

'Wine?' His voice was gruff. It sent a shiver right through her.

'No.' Hers was barely more than a whisper.

With a low growl, he closed the distance between them, his arms snapping around her as he pulled her into his chest, a cage of bone and muscle locking her in place, pressing her to him.

She felt like a candle, consumed by the flame of his need as he kissed her, his mouth urgent and demanding, and she melted into him, wanting this as much as he.

When he broke the connection and bent to scoop her into his arms and carry her off to bed, all conscious thought fled, as Carla made love to him with her body, her heart, and her soul.

CHAPTER NINE

It was amazing how quickly one could get used to something, Carla thought as she stepped out of the house on Hazel Road and locked the door. In the two weeks since she'd moved into the house in Picklewick, she had become very used to it indeed, and she'd even begun to feel as though she'd lived there forever.

Slipping the keys into her bag, she walked swiftly down the road, her heels tapping on the pavement. The noise made her frown, and her feet didn't appreciate the unaccustomed court shoes either. They weren't used to wearing them. They were more used to being encased in trainers these days.

As she made her way to the bus stop, Carla tugged self-consciously at the hem of her newly acquired jacket. She also wasn't used to wearing office-type attire, having become accustomed to jeans, tee shirts and hoodies. They were the only items of clothing she had brought with her when she'd fled Birmingham for the farm on Muddypuddle Lane over a month ago – apart from two dresses in case she went somewhere nice (like Otto's restaurant, for instance) and a pair of shorts should the weather be nice enough to warrant getting her legs out. So in order to attend an interview with the temp service in Thornbury, she'd had to scour the rails of Picklewick's charity shop for something suitable to wear.

She had also become very used to living in Picklewick. However, it wasn't the ideal place to set down new roots. The village was too quiet, and despite not wanting to live in a city again, she would like somewhere a little livelier. Besides, rental properties in Picklewick were more expensive than those in Thornbury. She knew this, because she'd checked.

Carla hadn't mentioned any of this to Ashton, and Dulcie thought Carla was mad not to tell him, but Carla's reasons were valid. She didn't want their relationship and the fact that she had fallen for him, to colour her decision – because she wasn't doing this for him, or for them. She was doing it for herself.

Anyway, all this was purely speculative, a plan in place in case the meeting with HR didn't go in her favour. Charlie, her union rep, would be attending it with her, and he seemed to think the outcome was cut and dried. Carla had forwarded copies of the contents of Anita's folder to him, and he had almost crowed with glee, declaring that the 'other party' (which was how he referred to Yale) wouldn't know what had hit him.

Carla wished she had Charlie's level of confidence. Quietly optimistic was as far as she would go.

Arriving at the bus stop, she joined the queue of people standing in the bus shelter and attempted to prepare herself for her interview. The temp agency had called it an 'informal chat,' but she knew it was more than that. She had to look the part, sound the part, and play the part if she wanted to be considered for the more lucrative placements.

But try as she might, her mind kept drifting to Ashton and she wondered whether he was in Picklewick at this very moment on his rounds.

She caught a glimpse of a red van, and her heart gave a lurch before settling back into its normal rhythm when she realised it wasn't a Royal Mail one.

She couldn't wait to see Ashton later, and she tingled at the thought. Since that fateful evening when they had made love for the first time, they'd hardly been able to keep their hands off each other, and Carla was most definitely in lust. The man was freakin' gorgeous, and he knew what to do with a woman between the sheets. And on the couch. And on the carpet once, but it had made the skin on her back sore so she wouldn't be doing that again in a hurry.

In case he was in the village, she shrank back and hid behind an elderly couple and their pull-along shopping trolley, and only when she was on the bus, did some of her tension evaporate.

Staring out of the window, she told herself to focus. She would have plenty of time to think about Ashton on the return journey. She needed to stop daydreaming and concentrate on what she was in Thornbury to achieve.

And whilst she was there, there was no harm in checking out what was available to rent.

'Got everything?' Ashton asked. He glanced at the suitcase by the bedroom door.

Carla scanned the room. 'I think so.'

He noticed she'd put fresh linen on the bed and he knew she wanted to leave Beth's rented house clean and tidy, but to him it felt like she was erasing every trace of herself, as though this was a hotel room and she was done with it. Done with **them**.

Yesterday had been bitter-sweet. They had spent her last day on the hill above the farm, taking photos, and when they'd spotted the stoat again, it had felt symbolic, her time in Picklewick bracketed by sightings of the little animal.

Last night he had held her until she'd drifted off to sleep. Unable to sleep himself, he'd lain beside her, listening to her soft breathing and trying not to think how lonely he would be without her.

Watching her pack this morning had been hard, so he'd sat in the garden with an untouched mug of coffee and waited until it was time to take her to the station.

With a heavy tread, Ashton carried her case out to the car while she did a final check, before locking up and posting the key through the letterbox. His heart squeezed painfully – far too soon they would be at the station, and he might never see her again.

She was subdued on the short journey to Thornbury, and he guessed she might be worried about her meeting tomorrow. She had tried to put it behind her for the most part over the past week or so, but he'd sensed it had been playing on her mind. He knew it would have played on his, if he had been in her position.

God, he would miss her.

Would she miss him?

In a way, he hoped not, because he didn't want Carla to experience the loneliness that he knew would be his lot after she was gone. He cared for her too much to think of her hurting.

Easing the car into a space in the station's car park, he switched the engine off and got out. 'Do you want me to wait with you until the train arrives?' he asked.

'Ashton....' Her expression was unreadable. She shook her head.

He sighed and opened his arms. Carla stepped into them, and he held her close for as long as he could, her head on his chest, his nose in her hair as he breathed in her scent.

Eventually, she pulled away to stare into his eyes, and he cupped her face with his hands.

'It'll be okay,' he said.

Then he kissed her one last time.

He hadn't fought for her. That was the only thing Carla could think of as she boarded the train. Ashton had let her go, had accepted that their relationship was over without so much as a murmur.

It hurt. A lot.

Did it alter her plans to return to Picklewick? Possibly.

The interview with the temp agency the other day had gone well, despite her honesty regarding the uncertainty around her current employment.

Beth had told her that she could stay in the house in Picklewick until she sorted out more permanent accommodation in Thornbury, and her mum had insisted on gifting Carla her car, so she had everything lined up. All she had to do was make the decision.

She had tried so hard not to let it hinge on Ashton, but how could it not since she was in love with him?

Ah, yes, the woman who had arrived in Muddypuddle Lane determined not to get entangled in another relationship, had well and truly lost her heart.

The journey to Birmingham seemed interminable, but eventually she trundled her case into the hall, the sound of her footsteps in the empty house echoing the emptiness inside her.

Can I come over? I need to see you.

Ashton read the message for a second time. Why did Lacey need to see him? What could they possibly have to talk about? He hadn't had any contact with her since she'd told him they were over, apart from seeing her in the Tex-Mex restaurant a couple of weeks ago, so why did she suddenly need to see him now?

His blood ran cold as a possible reason leapt into his mind. Could she be pregnant?

Ashton closed his eyes and breathed deeply, willing away the panic.

He would have been over the moon if she had told him this three months ago, but they weren't together any longer and the thought of being a single dad and estranged from his baby's mother, filled him with dread.

When? His response was terse.

Today?

I'm at home

20 mins ok?

It wasn't okay, but he had to know why Lacey wanted to see him.

Ashton snorted in derision. Be careful what you wish for, he thought. He had been scared of being lonely now that Carla had gone, but if Lacey was carrying his child, very soon he wouldn't have time to feel lonely.

What a bloody mess.

He went in search of something alcoholic, guessing they both might need some fortification, before remembering that pregnant women probably shouldn't drink.

He tried to recall what Lacey had been drinking in the restaurant, but all he could see was the look on her face. Had she known then that she was pregnant? If so, it would explain her odd expression.

When the doorbell rang, he flinched. Here goes, he thought, steeling himself. If she was indeed pregnant, he wanted to be part of his child's life and was fully prepared to fight for that.

Lacey was standing on the step, looking as lovely as always. A little tired perhaps, but if his suspicion was correct, it was to be expected.

'Can I come in?' she asked.

'Sure.' He held the door open, her familiar perfume wafting over him as she stepped inside. She appeared nervous, and he didn't blame her. He would be nervous, too.

Hell, he **was** nervous.

'Tea?' he asked.

'Can I have a glass of water?'

'Of course.' He poured one for her and one for himself, despite preferring something stronger, then sat down and gestured for her to sit.

She perched on the end of the sofa. 'I've, um... I don't know how to say this.'

Ashton waited.

'I think I've made a mistake.'

'You think... **What?**'

'Okay, I know I've made a mistake. I should never have broken up with you. I wasn't thinking straight.'

'Pardon?' He was struggling to get his head around what she was saying.

'I still love you, Ashton.'

'What?' he repeated incredulously. This wasn't what he'd expected her to say.

'Can we try again?'

'Me and you?'

She nodded, her head bowed.

'You want us to try again?' He couldn't believe he was hearing this.

'Yes.' Her voice was small.

'Why? You think I'm boring.'

'No, I don't. Honestly, I don't. I shouldn't have said it. I didn't mean it. Please Ash, I've made a terrible mistake. I've been so lonely without you, and I miss you so much. Please give us another chance. **Please.'**

Ashton closed his eyes. Not too long ago he would have given everything he had to hear those very words, but now there was Carla... Carla, who had walked out of his life, leaving a gaping hole of loss and loneliness.

'I saw you, Ash.' Lacey broke into his anguished thoughts. 'Outside the station earlier with that woman. You looked so sad. Do you love her? Am I too late?'

He **did** love her. With a stab to the chest, he finally admitted that he had fallen head over heels in love with Carla.

But Carla was no longer here. Lacey was, and he still cared for her.

Was it enough?

Carla was conscious that she didn't look her best for this meeting. She was wearing a suit and heels, but there were shadows under her eyes and her face was pale.

Nervously, her heart in her mouth, she entered the building and made for the lifts, hoping no one would see her as she slunk inside. And by 'no one', she meant Yale. He wouldn't be at this meeting, but he would probably be in his office, and she dreaded bumping into him.

It wasn't like a court of law, where the accuser and the accused would be in the same room. This was a disciplinary hearing, after which HR would make its decision as to her future with the company. She would have the right to appeal, and take it to an independent tribunal, but if this meeting didn't go in her favour, she didn't think she had the will to fight. Just like Anita Campbell, she would meekly accept her fate and walk away.

Her union rep was waiting for her, and they were shown into a small office for a private discussion before she was called. Although she'd met with Charlie online, she hadn't met him in person, and he looked younger in the flesh. He also looked confident. She wished she felt the same.

'Are you okay?' he asked.

Carla nodded. She felt sick and shaky, and her mouth was dry. She just wanted to get this over with.

The door opened.

'If you'd like to follow me,' a woman said. Carla recognised her as Mrs Bissett's assistant.

Three people sat around a large table, laptops open, pads and pens at the ready. Carla and Charlie took a seat, Carla barely listening to the preliminaries of why the meeting had been called.

Mrs Bissett had just launched into a spiel about the seriousness of the allegation against her, when Charlie interrupted. 'Can I stop you there?'

Mrs Bissett raised an eyebrow as he pushed a folder across the desk.

'You might want to take a look at this before you go any further,' he said. He got to his feet. Carla did the same. 'You'll need some time to peruse the contents, so we'll wait outside.'

To Carla, the wait was torture.

However, the outcome of the meeting wasn't.

Ashton, Anita and Charlie had been right – Yale hadn't had a leg to stand on.

'That's wonderful news!'

Everyone Carla had spoken to – her mother, Vicky, Dulcie, Anita – had all said the same thing when she'd phoned them as soon as she'd got home. They were thrilled she had been reinstated, that the dark cloud hanging over her had been lifted, that her job was safe, and she would be returning to her desk tomorrow.

Or would she?

She hadn't decided what she was going to do. She knew what she wanted to do, but that wasn't the same as doing it.

Carla's hand hovered over the phone. There was one person who she had yet to call.

Ashton.

She checked the time. Ten minutes past one. He would still be doing his rounds. He might be in his van, driving. In fact, he probably was, so rather than phone, she would send him a message. It was safer. He could read it at his convenience.

God, that sounded so formal, and formal was the last thing she wanted.

She picked the phone up, then put it down again.

Was it too early for wine? A celebratory glass? This didn't feel like a celebration, though.

It felt flat. Meaningless. A hollow victory. And it was that realisation which was the deciding factor.

The phone was in her hand again – it was time to make another call.

Post redirected? **Tick.**

Fridge emptied? **Tick.**

Windows locked? **Tick.**

Everything turned off? **Tick.**

Carla had a final scout around the house, hoping she hadn't forgotten anything. The past couple of hours had been a blur of frenetic activity, but once she'd made the decision there seemed little point in putting it off until tomorrow. By tonight she would be in Picklewick, and her new life could begin.

It felt strange to leave the house she'd lived in since she was a child, the house she would always refer to as home. For the time being, she was moving into Beth's rented house in the village until she found somewhere suitable in Thornbury. Living in the small market town was the perfect compromise. It wasn't as big as a city, yet neither was it too rural. And after speaking to the temp agency earlier, she already had a job lined up for Monday.

Carla wandered through every room, drinking each one in, before scolding herself for being silly. It wasn't as though she would never see this place again. As soon as her mum was back from the Caribbean, Carla would pay her a visit.

Locking up, she hurried to the car, now eager to be on her way. A new life beckoned, and she couldn't wait for it to begin. Whether Ashton would be in it remained to be seen.

She hoped with all her heart that he **would.**

It was late. Late for Ashton, but not late for most people. He had work in the morning and should be in bed, but unfortunately, he couldn't settle. Thoughts and images whirled through his mind, spinning like a merry-go-round. Except there was nothing merry about them.

He had been glad to see the back of yesterday (saying goodbye to Carla at the train station had been so hard), but today hadn't proved to be any better. He had waited in vain for a call from her, even if it was just to tell him the outcome of her meeting. However, his phone had remained silent: no call, no message.

Her lack of contact convinced him it was over. She was back in her old life, her time in Picklewick now nothing but a memory. And that hurt. He'd thought they had something special, but he'd clearly been kidding himself. And despite vowing not to let anyone else into his heart, he had fallen in love. The pain he'd felt when Lacey had dumped him was nothing compared to the heartache he felt now.

Wryly, he supposed he should be thankful to Carla for showing him what love truly was. He supposed he should also be thankful to Lacey for turning down his marriage proposal. If she hadn't, he would have spent his life not knowing how love really felt.

It was both beautiful and awful.

Right now, awful was winning hands down.

His mobile beeped, and he hoped it wasn't Lacey. She hadn't taken his rejection well yesterday, and her tears had tugged on his heartstrings, but he'd held firm. It wouldn't be fair on either of them if he settled for second best.

Ashton looked at his phone, and his heart lurched violently.

Carla. Finally.

Are you awake? she messaged.

Yes

He waited for a call, or even a reply. And he waited, and waited.

The ring of his doorbell made him jump. Who could this be at just gone nine on a Friday evening? It wouldn't be his parents, because they knew better. Anyway, they were still touring Scotland in their camper van and would be away for a few more weeks yet.

He heaved his weary body out of the chair and went to answer it.

Carla was outside.

Ashton blinked, then squinted. It was her; he wasn't imagining it. 'I didn't think you were coming back,' he said.

'I wasn't sure, either. Yet here I am.'

'How did the meeting go?' He wanted to scoop her into his arms and kiss her until she begged him to stop, but he couldn't move.

'Can I come in? If it's not too late?'

It would never be too late for Carla.

'Of course.' He stood aside for her to enter, then closed the door behind her.

She said, 'I was going to leave it until tomorrow to see you, but I couldn't wait.' She hesitated and he got the impression that she didn't intend to stay long.

The thought of her leaving when she'd only just got here, made his chest hurt.

'I've had a formal apology from HR,' she continued. 'And Yale has been suspended.'

'That's brilliant news. I told you, didn't I?'

'You did.'

'When do you start back?'

'I don't.'

Anger reared its head at the injustice of it. 'They can't do that!'

'**They** didn't. **I** did. I resigned.'

'You did what?' He was flabbergasted. Ashton sank into the armchair he hadn't long vacated. He didn't think he could take any more surprises today.

'That's not all,' she said. 'I'm moving to Picklewick.'

'For good?' Dear lord, he needed a stiff drink.

'Only until I find somewhere to rent in Thornbury.'

'But, what— I don't—' He inhaled deeply. His heart was racing, and he felt a little lightheaded.

'I've fallen in love with the place,' she said. 'Just like Dulcie. And just like Dulcie, I've fallen in love with a local chap. He's a bit boring, talks about image sensors and apertures quite a lot, and he's obsessed with taking photos—'

Ashton leapt to his feet and swept her into his arms, stopping her words with his mouth. Her lips parted, and she sank into his embrace with a whimper that sent him delirious with desire.

But before he whisked her off to bed and made love to her for the rest of the night, there was something he had to say.

'I love you,' he murmured gently.

Carla was more forthright. 'I bloody hope so! Now shut up and kiss me.'

And because Ashton was a thoroughly nice guy and he didn't like to disappoint a lady, he did just that!

Carla had never before reached the 'meet the parents' stage in a relationship, mainly because she'd never felt invested enough.

She was invested now alright, and she couldn't wait to meet Ashton's. They were away, but his grandmother lived in Picklewick's care home and that's where they were headed right now.

Her name was Nancy and Carla hoped they would get along.

An old lady with pink hair was seated in a wingback chair next to a large picture window with a view of the mountain above Muddypuddle Lane. Her lined face creased into a beautiful smile when she saw Ashton, and he bent to kiss her on the cheek.

She brushed him away, as eyes the same hue as Ashton's settled on Carla.

Carla squirmed under her scrutiny. 'Hi.'

'Come closer, let me look at you. So, you're the young lady who has stolen my grandson's heart. I hope you don't break it.'

Carla could feel Ashton's anxious gaze on her, but she didn't flinch. Nancy's directness was refreshing. 'I won't.'

'How do I know that?'

'Because he has mine.'

'Good answer.' Nancy patted the arm of the chair next to hers. 'Sit here. I want to know all about you. Ashton, fetch tea. I take it, you drink tea?'

'Of course,' Carla replied.

'Do you eat biscuits?'

'Loads of them.'

'What's your favourite?'

'Gosh, now you're asking. Something with chocolate on, I think.'

Nancy said, 'Ashton, bring a plate of biscuits while you're at it. This could take a while.'

The two women watched him leave, both of them with love in their eyes.

Then Nancy turned her attention back to Carla. 'He's such a nice boy. They don't make many like that these days. You want to keep hold of him.'

Carla leant towards the old lady and put her hand on Nancy's age-spotted one. 'Don't worry, I intend to.'

And she meant it!

There are loads more large print books in the Muddypuddle Lane series. Available at all good book stores, or ask your local library.

About Etti

Etti Summers is the author of wonderfully romantic fiction with happy ever afters guaranteed.

She is also a wife, a mum, a pink gin enthusiast, a veggie grower and a keen reader.

www.ingramcontent.com/pod-product-compliance
Lightning Source LLC
Chambersburg PA
CBHW050600190726
48283CB00007B/2214